A CIRCLE OF CELEBRATIONS

The Complete Edition

A CIRCLE OF CELEBRATIONS

The Complete Edition

HOLIDAY STORIES BY

JODY LYNN NYE

New York Times bestselling author

WordFire Press
Colorado Springs, Colorado

A CIRCLE OF CELEBRATION

Trade Paperback ISBN: 978-1-61475-287-5
Case Laminate Hardcover ISBN: 978-1-68057-577-4

Cover design by Janet McDonald

Art Director Kevin J. Anderson

Cover artwork images by Dollar Photo Club

Book Design by RuneWright, LLC
www.RuneWright.com

Published by
WordFire Press, an imprint of
WordFire, Inc.
PO Box 1840
Monument CO 80132

Kevin J. Anderson & Rebecca Moesta, Publishers

WordFire Press Trade Paperback Edition December 2015

wordfirepress.com

Contents

FOREWORD

Celebrations help us to mark moments in time that are meaningful, some for religious reasons, others cultural and historical. From time to time, I've written about holidays, from many points of view, in this world, in another; in the past, present, and future. What they have in common is that we choose to come together for these festive events to discover joy and mystery.

Four of these stories I wrote to perform aloud for the audience at the Twilight Tales reading series in Chicago. Four were commissioned for anthologies, and the rest are original stories for this volume. They are all collected here for the first time. I hope you'll enjoy them.

Happy holidays!

Jody Lynn Nye
November, 2015

Valentine's Day

Myth Lonelyhearts

I looked around the ruffled-sided tent at the array of cards, statues, satin pillows, toys, candies, and an array of more adult items, the use of some I had to guess at. Every single item had been made, dyed, or painted red, white, or brilliant, eye-burning pink.

I glanced at Aahz. Like me, the Pervect hesitated on the threshold.

"Come in, come in!" exclaimed the Deveelish proprietor, Valentinius. Red-skinned with hooved feet and a long, skinny tail like all of his kind, he had a long, narrow face and high-arched eyebrows. He beckoned us in with a flick of his beautifully manicured talons, albeit shooting a look of resigned disdain at my companion. Short of stature but broad in the shoulder, Aahz had green-scaled skin, yellow eyes, and batwing ears. He hailed from a dimension called Perv, which meant his kind were called Pervects, if you liked them, or Perverts, if you didn't. They had such an interdimensional reputation for questionable behavior that even after years of knowing him and other Pervects I had no idea if it was earned. Valentinius was no doubt concerned for the welfare of his stock and possibly his employees. I, as a tall, skinny, blond-haired Klahd, never posed a threat to anyone in Deva, a dimension that possessed far more magikal potential than mine ever dreamed existed. "Come and examine the wares. Affection Day is coming! Your special someone will be expecting a gift from here. You know it. I know it! So, buy already!"

"What the hell," Aahz said, plunging into the first aisle. "C'mon, Skeeve."

"Aahz?" I asked, all but stumbling in behind him. "Do you have a special someone? You've never mentioned one."

"One?" Aahz turned back to me, his four-inch-long pointed teeth set more in a rictus than a grin. "I have a dozen, and they'll all be furious if I don't come up with something that tells them how I feel about them." He waggled his scaly eyebrows at me.

"How can they be special if there are a dozen of them?" I asked. My own experiences with women had been largely unsuccessful, or so I could recall. The women that I cared about most in the world were friends, not lovers—at least so far.

"Weeeellll," Aahz said, narrowing one big yellow eye with an expression that spoke of annoyed embarrassment. "None of them knows about the others, so to each, she's my one-and-only."

"Gosh." It was all I could find to say. I admired Aahz. I had no idea how he could juggle a lot of relationships like that without getting them confused. Or in a lot of trouble.

"Try a sweet, young Klahd?" a female Deveel asked, shoving a pink and white box under my nose. "Free samples. Guaranteed harmless and delicious. Just the thing to show your warm sentiment on Affection Day!"

I peered into the container. Nestled in individual paper nests were solid, irregular ovals of dark brown-red sweets with narrow stripes of pink daubed on them in random directions. I'd cut up enough carcasses to know what I was looking at.

"Eyugh," I said, wrinkling my nose. "Heart-shaped candy?"

The Deveel snarled at me, sharp white teeth showing vividly in her deep red face. "Get with the spirit of the day, Klahd. You're supposed to show someone that you'd let them eat your heart if it would make them happy."

The heart seemed to be a common theme in the crowded tent. Shoppers considered all kinds of items featuring that vital organ:

cards, scrolls, rings, necklaces, garters, bottles of potions, philters, and spells. Over a half of the not inconsiderable floor space was devoted to racks and tables of embarrassing-looking garments for all genders and body types. I had never worn anything like that myself, but I had seen a number of them among the plethora of wedding presents given to my former apprentice, Massha. I had no doubt, considering the healthy relationship she had with retired general Hugh Badaxe that they had made good use of the gifts.

"Oh, yeah!" Aahz crowed. He headed toward a clothesline from which hung bits and pieces of fabric in the obligatory red, pink, and white. None of them looked large enough to clothe a Gnome, let alone a Pervect. Then I recalled the tiny swimsuits that Bunny and the other beauty contestants had donned (for a brief look (see what I did there?), consult the compelling tale, "Myth Congeniality," in *Myth-Told Tales*, a collection of brilliant stories of conniving, derring-do, and camaraderie), and the items no longer looked too scanty. But the thought of putting Bunny, Tananda, or any of my female friends into one made my heart pound furiously. I began to understand the candies offered by the Deveel clerk.

"So, how may I take your money?" Valentinius sidled up beside me. He thrust an armload of items into my hands. "What do you need? Flowers? A satin pillow, perhaps? The sentiment embroidered on this one is bespelled to change with your loved one's mood." I glanced at the pink oval. It said, "Drop dead, you creep!"

"Uh, no, thanks," I said, shoving them back. Valentinius flicked a wrist. Instead of dropping to the floor, they hovered around him, spinning so I could see every angle.

"What sort of item were you hoping to find for your very special someone?" he asked, fluttering his long eyelashes.

The phrase had begun to irk me. "I don't have a special someone!" I said, with perhaps more heat than was necessary. Valentinius didn't take it amiss; no Deveel worth his salt would take shouting as a cue to exit an argument. If anything, it indicated the beginning of a bargain.

"Well, if you *don't*, I have powders and other items you can use to *make* someone interested in you. Bracelets? Rings? I've got a spray that you can use to perfume a room to attract just the right person. Want to give it a try? Only two coppers per spritz."

I had a brief vision of having hordes of strange people charging toward me with lust in their eyes, and shuddered.

"No, thanks. I can come up with my own bad ideas."

"Are you calling my merchandise *bad ideas*?" he shrieked, raising his voice so high that shoppers for three rows around turned to look. "It figures that a Klahd can't tell true romance from heartburn!"

"Hey, I'll know it when I see it," I protested, albeit weakly.

"Kid! Stop playing around!" Aahz marched over and shoved a hand between my shoulder blades, aiming me toward the clothes racks. The Deveel gave us both a disgusted look and sauntered away. Not a yard from us, he latched onto the arm of a bright-pink Imp matron.

"Darling, you don't want that! It doesn't match anything in this entire dimension!"

"C'mon," Aahz said. "I'm afraid of what you'll end up buying if you don't stay close to me."

"Okay, Aahz," I said. To tell the truth, I was relieved. Even though I had lived in the Bazaar for years, I had yet to explore every corner, tent, and booth. Adding to the confusion was the fact that shops routinely disappeared from one location and reappeared in another, often under a new name, although less often with a new owner or manager. I'd been fooled more than once by patronizing a business only to learn that it belonged to a Deveel who had tried to outrun his reputation for unusually shady dealing by relocating. To my best recollection, I had never seen this one before. "Has this shop been here long?"

"It's a pop-up," Aahz said. "Seasonal merchandise. It's like the Festival of Hamsters. In between, no one wants to see the stuff. You can see why."

I watched other shoppers, but I really couldn't tell what they were buying. The baskets were bespelled so that anything tossed into them became invisible. Aahz was just as cagey about his purchases.

Every so often, he darted a glance around to see if anyone was watching him, then grabbed something off one of the long tables. I eyed the display, which appeared to be all garments in pink and white, decorated—no, *festooned* with lace and stretchy straps. I had not seen the size of the item that Aahz had shoved into his shopping basket, so I couldn't even make a guess as to the race of the one-and-only for whom he had bought it. He stopped and eyed one table in the crowded tent. Though they were tinted pink and white, the items on display looked like implements of torture. Owing to a recent visit to a professional torturer (see the whole sordid story in *Myth-Fits*, coming to a reputable or disreputable seller of literature near you), I had some uncomfortable familiarity with such things.

One apparatus struck me as unusually odd. It consisted eight or ten broad, various-sized loops of white leather all bound together with stretchy pink elastic, chains and matching padlocks, each with a heart incised on it. I picked it up.

"Hey, Aahz, what's this for?"

With a long-suffering sigh, he took it out of my fingers and dropped it back on the table.

"That, you absolutely do not want to know," he said. "Look, it's Affection Day. Why don't you pick out something for people you like?"

"I've never heard of Affection Day," I protested. "And I don't have a special someone, like Valentinius said."

"You have a bunch of special someones," Aahz said, with a shake of his head. "You just ain't dating any of them. Get something PG-rated for them. Go look over there." He pointed to a group of tables where a Deveel, a handful of Imps, and two Centaurs were browsing. "Scram. I don't want to have to keep explaining what I'm buying."

The half-horse, half-Klahd beings made way as I sidled up to the table to examine the wares. A female Centaur, wearing nothing but her long chestnut-colored tresses over her bosom, was sorting through a sheaf of colorful little books. One of them was called *The True Story of Affection Day*. I picked up a similar volume and browsed through it. What I read made me sputter in outrage.

"Is this right?" I asked the Centaur female. "This holiday was made up by Deveel merchants to sell candy? It's phony?"

She smiled at me, showing a mouthful of long, horsy teeth.

"That's right, Klahd," she said, with a nickering laugh. "But many of us have adapted it for ourselves to tell our loved ones that we value them."

"But what about all that other stuff? The charmed portraits? The Miss Lonelyhearts contests? Those?" I pointed to the racks of questionable garments. "That's not candy."

She gave a nickering laugh and patted me on the shoulder.

"You are young, Klahd. Sweet things come in many guises."

I felt my cheeks burn. I wasn't *that* young!

"Grizzle grum nang dabbit marn flandifulation!"

One of the clothing displays gave a massive heave and fell towards me. I had just enough time to ready a spell that kept the mass of satin and leather from tumbling down over the Centaur and me. The female trotted out of the way of the bondage avalanche, holding her basket. I tried to make the rack stand upright, but the person swearing must have been tangled up inside it.

Valentinius strode toward me, *tut-tutting* furiously.

"Did you knock that over?" he demanded.

"No!" I said. "I'm holding it up!"

He glanced past me at the clutter on the floor and sniffed. "Very badly, I see."

I was willing to do favors out of common decency, but such a thing was often lost on Deveels. I let my spell lapse.

CRASH!

The garments spilled in every direction, leaving a large, black-bearded, leather-clad Klahd lying in their midst, only this leather was well-worn military-grade armor—not a bad choice, considering that shopping in the Bazaar during the end-of-season sales could result in mortal wounds. He clutched a handful of pink satin to his chest. I recognized him in an instant. It was retired Possiltum general Hugh Badaxe. His face flushed scarlet as he met my gaze.

"Another Klahd!" the Deveel said, flicking a fingernail. The general swung up into the air as if he weighed no more than the wispy feathers that decorated the garment in his hand. "We request that you do not use the merchandise until after you have purchased it!" He walked purposefully toward the tent's door, preparing to fling Badaxe into the dusty, sun-drenched street.

"Wait!" I said, jumping into the Deveel's path. "Don't you know who that is?"

"No, who is it?" Valentinius asked, raising one thin eyebrow.

Badaxe waved a frantic hand at me. I gulped. If he was buying something in the Bazaar instead of on Klah, he probably wanted it kept a secret.

"That's my uncle Harv," I said. "He's here to make a big purchase. A BIG purchase."

"Oh," Valentinius said. He closed his fingers, and Badaxe dropped to the floor with an audible thud. "Fine. But he's handled the size XXXXXXL Cupy panties, so he'll have to buy them, too."

"No problem," I said.

"Three gold pieces."

"One silver," I countered. "After all, he's handled them now. They're used. You couldn't sell them to a Cupy now if you wanted to."

"Two gold pieces."

"Two silver. That's my final offer."

Valentinius looked from me to the general, who had risen to his feet with what dignity he could muster. He was half again the Deveel's height and at least three times his weight, although physical stature meant little in dimensions where magik might be involved. Valentinius showed a mouthful of sharp-pointed white teeth.

"Five silver. Not a copper less. It will take me such a loooooong time to clear up the mess you left!"

"I'll pay it," Badaxe said, reaching into his belt pouch. "Thanks anyhow, nephew." He dropped the coins into Valentinius's palm, from which they disappeared faster than the merchandise in the shopping baskets. The Deveel flicked a hand at the display. It straightened itself out in a flash, all of the odd-looking garments hanging themselves in perfect order. Badaxe watched with a jaundiced eye. We both knew he'd overpaid to appease the Deveel.

"What are you doing here, *uncle*?" I asked in a low tone.

This big, muscular man had faced down armies against terrible odds, both in terms of enemy numbers and the parsimony of the kingdom treasurer, JR Grimble, but he almost trembled with nerves.

"Affection Day," he said. "I want to buy something for Massha. No, I *have* to buy her something."

"For a fake holiday?"

He made a face. "If you want to know the truth, she's upset with me."

"Why?" I asked.

The expression changed to one that he probably aimed at young recruits who had said something monumentally stupid.

"If I knew that, I would apologize and promise never to do it again. As it is," he added with a sigh, "I'm in the dark. She hasn't talked to me for a week. She hasn't even looked at me. That's not like her. We don't even...." His cheeks flushed. "Never mind, son. Need to know. It can't go on like this. The palace isn't that big. We keep running into each other, and people are starting to talk. You know the Queen's on her side. She could make it pretty miserable for me if she thinks I'm making Massha unhappy. So, I'm using Affection Day as an excuse to try and break through the barrier. My concern is that she'll throw my present back in my face."

I became worried. Massha was someone I cared about, too.

"Can I help?" I asked. He held up the handful of pink satin. I backed away a pace with my hands held up to ward it off. "I mean, I can't help you choose a gift. I'm not good at buying present for people."

"Oh, this?" Hugh looked at it with a faint air of embarrassment. "I thought she'd look good in it." He spread the garment out with both hands. It appeared to be a pair of tiny panties with little white feathered wings affixed at each hip. The wings fluttered.

"That?" I asked, in astonishment. Massha was a lady of monumental proportions, who favored harem pants and brief tops that left her broad stomach bare to help keep her cool. "That wouldn't cover very much of her, would it?"

Badaxe grinned. "That's kind of the idea, Skeeve. I love the way she looks. But I'm in pretty deep muck. If you've seen something else in here that she'd like better, I'm open to ideas."

"She collects jewelry, mostly magikal gizmos," I offered. "If I was going to buy her something it would be a device she doesn't have yet."

"I don't know a quarter of what her magik stuff does," Badaxe said glumly. "I had better stick to a present that shows her I'm sorry even if I don't know what I'm being sorry for."

"I'd be happy to run interference for you," I said. "Massha's been a good friend, as have you."

He eyed me with sideways speculation.

"Would you be willing to deliver gifts to her for me?" he asked.

"Sure." I knew the castle well. Massha occupied the position I had vacated as Court Magician to the Kingdom of Possiltum. She used my old offices, a majestic suite of rooms in the best tower. I also knew the honeymoon cottage that she and Badaxe had been given by the queen as a wedding present.

"Great!" A jubilant Badaxe grabbed me by the arm and dragged me toward the racks of clothing.

"Wait a minute!" I protested. "I didn't say I'd dress up!"

"If you're an Affection Day messenger, you need to wear the uniform," Badaxe said. "Are you a soldier in this being's army, or aren't you?"

"What's going on?" Aahz appeared from the midst of the racks. Hastily, he shoved a bright green and black satin corset into his basket, where it disappeared.

"Hey, Aahz," Badaxe said, his face dropping into a relatively neutral expression. He and Aahz had a cordial relationship. As hard as I had tried, I couldn't get them to warm to each other. "Skeeve just offered to do me a favor."

"What kind of favor?" Aahz asked, always mistrustful of my ability to negotiate on my own behalf. All right, most of the time he was right, but I was pretty sure that I had agreed to a fairly innocuous task.

"Affection Day messenger," I said. "Badaxe needs me to bring some presents to Massha."

Aahz grinned, showing all of his teeth.

"And you need the uniform," he said, hooking his hand into my other arm. "Well, come on, partner. After you drop the general's parcels off, I've got a few addresses I'd like you to visit."

"Uh … okay."

"He looks like a medium long," Badaxe said, running an

experienced eye up and down my lanky frame.

"No problem." Aahz plunged into the racks of clothing.

O O O

"Are you sure I need all of this stuff?" I asked, looking at myself in a red-framed magik mirror that showed my front, sides and back in rapid sequence, over and over again. I stood on a hovering disk at one side of the shop. My own clothes were in a heap on the floor. I now wore a knee-length red tunic over white trousers, belted with a leather belt from which hung a quiverful of pink feathers. Over one shoulder, a shining white bow was slung by its slack string. Over the other was a huge, empty pink satchel. "What are the bow and arrows for? Do I have to shoot my way out of the room?"

"They're traditional symbols of Affection Day," Valentinius said, fussing around me. "You shoot the arrows of love at the heart of the person you want to win."

"How is a fatal assault romantic?" I asked, aghast. This was definitely not a holiday on Klah. "Am I missing something?"

The Deveel stood up and put his hands on his hips and sent an exasperated look to Badaxe. "Are you sure you want him for your messenger? He doesn't seem to understand anything."

"He's fine," Aahz snarled. The Deveel backed off, not eager to face off against a Pervect, even in his own shop. He didn't know that Aahz had no magikal powers. "Get on with the fitting. You're wasting time."

"Yes, yes."

Valentinius pointed a sharp nail at the pink boots he had had me don. From the heels sprang little white wings. To my surprise, when they fluttered they lifted me right off the disk. He snapped his fingers. A short cylindrical box about a foot across rushed to his hands. He pried off the lid and extracted, from a tissue-paper nest within, a red hat. I was not too fond of hats, which was lucky because I hardly ever needed one in the desert climate. I had also never been noted for my sartorial style. Most of my clothes had been picked out by Bunny, currently president of M.Y.T.H., Inc., once she had managed to convince me that I was a self-inflicted fashion victim. But even I wouldn't have tried on, let alone bought, the topper that Valentinius brandished at me. It had a flat, round crown with a silver bill that stuck out over the forehead. The band that ran around the brim had a pattern of jewels arranged in stripes of pink, red and white that flashed in sequence. Sticking up over one ear was a long, fluffy pink feather with a jeweled clip. The end of the feather bobbed up and down as if in time to the flashing gems.

"No," I said, firmly. "Not if my life depended on it. I'll wear it without the hat."

"But you have to!" Hugh Badaxe said, desperation in his eyes.

"Why does it matter?" I asked. "I'll travel back to Klah, flutter over to the castle, present your gifts to Massha, then go visit Aahz's … friends. I don't need the hat."

"It's part of the spell," Valentinius said, exasperated. He flipped a hand. The hat shot toward me. I ducked, but it clapped itself onto my head. I clawed at it, prying at the smooth felt. The hat almost cackled at me in triumph. I couldn't get it off. It held on tighter than my hair. The Deveel pointed at me. "Now, repeat after me:

In darkest day,
in bleakest night,
no lover shall escape delight.
No rain deter,
nor snow prevent me
bringing your Affection Day present."

"That's stupid," I said. "It doesn't really rhyme."

"Say it," Aahz gritted.

When the veins in his yellow eyes protruded, it meant Aahz was about to lose his temper. I repeated it.

The moment the last syllable left my lips, I felt magikal power surge downward from the hat and upward from the wings on my heels. The string of my bow vibrated in a higher and higher tone until my ears were pleading for mercy. I tried to fling away the parts of the costume, but they seemed to have become part of my body.

Aahz and Badaxe stuffed the contents of their shopping baskets into the pouch.

"One last thing," Badaxe said. He shoved aside a section of his breastplate, took one of the arrows out of my quiver, gritted his teeth, and plunged the arrow into his heart. I was aghast, but the arrow melted away, leaving no visible wound. The feathers fluttered to the floor. "That's so she knows I really love her."

"This is crazy!" I shouted, over the now deafening whine of the bowstring.

"Have a nice trip, partner," Aahz said. "Tell Massha hello for me."

"Thanks, Skeeve," Badaxe said.

I managed to choke out words in spite of the juddering.

"But how am I going to get back to …?"

Bamf!

"Yiiii!" I yelped, as I appeared in Klah, or, rather, high over it. In all the times we had traveled to my home dimension, we had always landed somewhere on the ground. For the first time, I arrived up in the sky. It took me a minute to get my bearings. I spun in mid-air, looking for landmarks. Below was thick forest. It ran unbroken in all directions except for a snaking line that I knew had to be a road. My eye followed it until I spotted pennants and banners floating from the conical tops of towers. One of them I knew almost as well as I knew my own name, since I had lived in it for several months. The castle! I leaned toward it.

The wings on my feet had been designed to keep me in the air, but not necessarily on an even keel.

"Whoa!"

I windmilled my arms, but I found myself flying upside down in the direction of the castle. The bag full of presents started to slip off my shoulder. I caught the strap just in time and hung onto it.

To save myself, I needed a supply of magik energy from force lines. In a dimension like Deva, they're everywhere, both underground and in the sky. In Klah, there were far fewer. I used my inner eye to scan for them. The nearest high-level one, a thin blue wavy arch, was miles away. Underground, I sensed a spiky red stripe zigzagging along almost parallel to the road. Aahz warned me to be cautious about the streams from which I drew power, but it was the only one handy.

Other than making my ears burn and my tongue vibrate, the power seemed pretty innocuous. I drew enough to fill my inner reserves. Once I'd done that, it was easy to flip myself upright and settle my bag over my shoulder.

"Wizard ho!"

"Prepare to defend!"

As I neared the edge of the forest, I spotted a number of men-at-arms in the small village that lay at the foot of the castle mount. I waved to them. Then, I realized they wouldn't recognize me. Skeeve the Magnificent, former court wizard, was an elderly and forbidding figure, with hollow eyes and a domelike skull, dressed in dark, mystical robes, not the ridiculous young blond Klahd in red wearing a glittering hat band and armed with a quiver of pink arrows.

The soldiers formed into three lines, each with crossbows aimed in my direction.

"No, wait!" I shouted. "I'm a friend! A friend of Massha's! Don't—!"

Too late, a flight of bolts shot in my direction. I spread my hands and created a force shield large enough to protect me and ducked behind it. The bolts hit the shield point-first and bounced off.

"Sorcery! Call for the wizard!" came another cry.

"No!" I shouted. The second volley came flying. One of the quarrels glowed blue. Putting the shield over my back, I spun and made back for the forest. The other bolts kept sailing in a straight line, but the blue quarrel followed me as I wove between the trees. It grew closer and closer. No amount of magik that I threw at it dispelled it or made it fall. It had to be one of Massha's gizmos.

I dodged between a couple of trees that were so close together that half of the plume on my hat rubbed off against the bark on my right. The bolt shot through the gap with ease. I made for an enormous black-leaved beechoak I spotted ahead of me. When I was a foot away, I dodged hard to the right. The bolt didn't correct its trajectory in time. It buried itself deep in the beechoak's trunk. A high-pitched tone began to rise from the tree. I put all the power I had left into thrusting myself away from it. I was less than twenty feet away when the beechoak exploded into a cloud of toothpicks.

Thousands of them peppered my back and legs.

"Agggh!"

I plunged toward the forest floor and gathered more power from the spiky force line. I used handfuls of the magik to remove all the prickly projectiles from my skin. This time, I'd make the approach to the castle in disguise.

O O O

"Delivery?" Massha asked, as the courtier leading me up the winding staircase to the Court Magician's tower introduced me. She eyed me up and down without a hint of recognition. The page hadn't known me, either. I had assumed the humble garb of a peddler's boy, with a homespun tunic that drooped to my knees and a peaked hood so large that it covered most of my face. I held my bulging delivery bag out toward her. "I'm not expecting any deliveries, and I'm not paying any cash on delivery, pal. You can take that back where it came from."

My former apprentice had not changed her attire or her attitude just because she had taken on a lofty position. She was as tough as an Impish bannock, at least on the outside. As it was high summer in Klah, which is to say that it wasn't as cold as usual, she had on a pair of floaty blue trousers and an ornate vest to match that bared her entire midriff. She wore velvet slippers embroidered in gold with the queen's crest. Her bright orange hair was pulled into a knot on the top of her head.

I pulled at my forelock, which I had made seem greasy and possibly infested with vermin.

"Your pardon, my lady, but it's just a gift."

"A gift?" Massha's eyes widened. "Get out! Go away!" She twisted a ring on her finger, and the door slammed in our faces.

"Wait!" I shouted, leaping forward to pound on the door. "Massha, it's me! Skeeve! Open up!"

Although his face twisted with revulsion at my oily and filthy appearance, the page darted his hands at me to pull me away from the Court Magician's door.

"Guards!" he shouted.

I dropped my disguise in favor of another one. The page gawked and dropped to one knee. "My lord Skeeve the Magnificent!"

"It's all right, Bodin," I said, in the sepulchral tones I had used while wearing that face.

Massha flung open the door. She enveloped me in a crush of soft flesh.

"Skeeve! I am so glad it's you!"

I dragged my face out of the expanse of her shoulder and gasped in a deep breath.

"What's the matter? Why are you so afraid of gifts?"

She glanced at the page. "You can go, Bodin."

"Yes, my lady."

Massha beckoned to me.

"Come on in. I need a glass of wine. The lady has had a hard day." The room had been redecorated since I had occupied it. It reflected Massha's taste and comfort, with plenty of storage for her assorted magikal gear. She floated—Massha preferred to hover by means of a magikal bracelet than to walk, wherever possible—to a table set between a couple of big, overstuffed chairs. With a flick of her wrist, she made the diamond-cut carafe rise into the air and decant shimmering burgundy wine into a pair of colored goblets. Massha settled herself in the larger of the two seats. One of the glasses picked itself off the table and wafted toward me. "Bottoms up," she said, hoisting her own drink.

Once the door closed behind me, I dropped my second disguise.

"Happy Affection Day," I said, holding the bag of presents toward her.

Massha's face paled.

"You—! You're working for *him*?"

Her fingers trembled and faltered. Her wineglass dropped out of her hand. I dove forward, reaching out with a handful of magikal force to keep it from hitting the ground. Some of the wine splashed on my clothes, but to be honest, I think it improved them.

"What's the matter?" I asked, handing her the glass. It was still about half full. I brushed at my front. "I know the outfit's horrible, but it was Hugh's idea."

"Hugh?" Massha asked, weakly. She downed the wine and poured herself another. A little color returned to her broad face. "Hugh sent you? Not *him*?"

I hurried to sit down beside her.

"Of course he did. He's worried about you. Now that I see you, I'm worried, too. What's going on?"

"Oh, Boss!" she said, bursting into sobs. She buried her head on my shoulder and cried. Feeling helpless at the rain of tears pouring down my neck, I patted her arm.

"Wait a minute," I said, sitting back as a thought struck me. "If you didn't think Hugh sent me, who do you think did it? What is it you're worried about? And why did the soldiers shoot at me when they saw me flying toward the castle? What's going on?"

Massha sighed. She plumped back in her chair and threw her head against the pillow.

"You know I wasn't a … spring chicken when you met me on Jahk, right?"

"Right," I said. "I'm getting used to practically everyone I know having had a full life before I met them."

She looked deeply into my eyes, as if trying to see if I was sparing her feelings. I wasn't. I spoke the absolute truth. Almost everyone whose opinion I valued had lifetimes more experience than I did. Degrees of age, beauty, or physical impressiveness didn't make much difference to me. After all, if beauty mattered, I wouldn't have gone into partnership with a Pervect, who embodied more nightmare traits than most Klahds could handle without a flaming torch or a crossbow at hand. I hadn't started out that way, but I had grown some wisdom in the past few years. I raised my eyebrows.

Massha smiled.

"You're the greatest, Boss," she said.

"Just tell me the whole story," I said.

She shrugged her huge shoulders. "Not much to tell. I had some love affairs over the years. Most of them weren't important. My track record wasn't that great. But there was one guy, Shilldon. I fell hard for him. We learned magik together, which was great until it turned out I was a better magician than he was. He … wasn't happy about that. I had a couple of good friends in those days. They didn't like him, but I was absolutely crazy about him. I *worshipped* him. I thought we were meant to be together forever. So did he, or so he said."

She paused and gazed toward the window. I noticed that the high, peaked casements had been shuttered and a board nailed across the heavy wooden blinds.

"What happened to him?"

"He … you don't have to know the details," she said. "I would rather not relive it. I was still in love with him, even though I knew I needed to get away. Those friends covered for me. I went to the far end of Jahk, where you met me. The team had an idea about my past. They said if Shilldon had ever shown up, they would beat the stuffing out of him if he laid a hand on me. Then, you took me on as your apprentice. That was the happiest day of my life until then. Up until I met Hugh." Her hard expression softened into pink-cheeked tenderness. I would have melted into a puddle if any girl had ever aimed that sweet wistful face toward me.

"But you haven't seen Shilldon in years," I said. "What's the problem?"

She floated up from her chair and sailed toward a small, black chest that was bound with bright copper bands. Through my inner eye, I saw that the metal shimmered with power. No one but Massha would have been able to touch it, let alone open it. She grabbed a handful of rolled parchments and brought them to me.

"He's here! He's been sending me messages. All the servants I asked say they didn't bring them. They just turn up in my quarters or up here in the tower. It's creeping me out."

"They're just letters," I said. "Why do they scare you so much?"

"Shilldon and I swore eternal love to each other. That's why I've been giving Hugh the cold shoulder about Affection Day. I'm afraid what would happen if someone hit me with a love arrow. And then you turned up with a bow. What can I do, Boss?"

I skimmed the scrolls. If I hadn't known they were notes from a real person, I would have thought they were pages from the kind of steamy novel that Bunny liked to read during her off hours. "I can't live without you!" "When you left me, my life was dreary, dark, over!" "Come back to me, so I can show you the true love that I know still burns within both our hearts!"

"Wow," I said, handing them back. "Do you know where he is?"

Massha drew forth from her capacious bosom an amber crystal ball and held it on one meaty palm. It began to glow. Within, instead of a picture or mystic symbols, was a veil of cloud. Massha shook her head.

"He's blocking me. That was one thing he could always do better than I could."

I started to pace. The white bow hit me in the leg at every step.

"I don't know. If a girl ran away from me, I'd assume she didn't want to see me anymore."

"That's the difference between you and someone like Shilldon," Massha said, watching me walk up and down. "You'd have let me go. It looks like he never gave up on getting me back. Once I was away from him, I saw how he had been keeping his thumb on me. I haven't thought about him in years."

"If that's true, then why won't you let me give you the gifts that Hugh sent you? I realize that the arrows are kind of barbaric."

"They're magikal," Massha explained, drawing one from the quiver and examining it with an expert's eye. "The legend is that they'll guide you to your one true love. What if it's not Hugh?" She shoved the arrow back into place.

I shook my head. "You're the best and strongest couple I know. How could you even think he's not your one true love?"

Massha crushed her hands together.

"But what if he's not? I can't tell you how I worshipped Shilldon. He's charismatic and gorgeous. I couldn't imagine my life without him—until the day that I could."

"Did he ever shoot Affection Day arrows at you when you were with him?" I asked.

"No. Shilldon said it wasn't necessary. He said we were fated to be together without little tricks."

I smacked my fist into my other palm. "Maybe he was afraid to find out that you weren't. Forgive me for saying it, because I am the last person you want to ask about relationships, but it sounds like you were fascinated and intimidated by him. Not in love."

Tears welled up in her eyes. She dabbed at them with the edge of her filmy blue sleeve.

"Thanks, Boss."

I toyed with the pink feathers.

"It sounds to me like the best thing you can do is let me use an arrow on you. Once you have it confirmed that your true love is Hugh, Shilldon will have to go away."

She shook her head, wide-eyed.

"No. I can't take that risk. What if the arrows say that Hugh's not the one for me? I'd have to leave Klah. I couldn't hurt him like that."

"It would hurt him more if you went away. Let him fight for you. Let him take on this Shilldon."

"No, way, Boss. He can't fight a magician! That's why … It's killing me, Skeeve. I've got to end it. I just don't know how."

"Then, let me help," I said. "Stay in here. Don't let anyone else in."

"How will I know it's you?"

I grinned. "I'll light a candle."

O O O

Queen Hemlock of Possiltum looked me up and down with cool amusement. A woman in her early middle years with dark hair shot through with silver and possessed of an air that spoke of absolute authority, she sat, or rather, reclined, across the arms of her throne, with her gown hiked up to expose her legs. They were her best feature. At my request, she sent away all of her courtiers except for a handmaiden who filled the queen's goblet with blood-red wine. She didn't offer me any. I'd have been foolish to accept it if she had. We weren't precisely friends, but we weren't exactly enemies. At her side stood JR Grimble, Chancellor of the Exchequer and my former supervisor. He liked me even less than Hemlock did.

"You look stupid," Hemlock told me.

"I know," I said, with a shrug. "I am doing a favor for a couple of friends."

"It's a good thing few will recognize my former Court Magician," she said, examining her nails. "To humiliate the office is to humiliate me. You've seen the inside of my dungeon, but I've added a few things since you were last in it. Would you like to test out some of the torture equipment? My jailors would love to try them on you."

I waved a casual hand.

"I'll skip the tour, your majesty. I'm just here to help Massha."

That got her attention.

"In that getup? How?"

I glanced at the serving girl. "I'm reluctant to expose another magician's secrets in front of … outsiders."

"Enchant her as you please," Hemlock said, with an offhand wave. The girl trembled and ducked her head. "Turn her into a statue. Just get on with it. I have an audience with a trade delegation shortly."

I met the girl's eyes.

"I won't hurt you," I said. "I'm just going to close off your ears for a few minutes."

She nodded without saying a word. In my mind's eye I saw the magik I sent her way packing a couple of big down pillows on either side of her head.

"Can you hear me?" I asked. Her wondering look told me she was puzzled as to where the sound had gone.

"Good," Hemlock said, curtly. "Get on with it."

I explained Massha's situation. When I began to detail the story of the past love, Hemlock swung her legs around and set her fists on her knees.

"Where is the son-of-a-Deveel?" she demanded. "I'll tear him to pieces. Show him to me!"

"I don't know where he is," I said. "He has to be in the castle grounds, if he's been bringing her letters without anyone seeing him. She's afraid for Hugh's sake more than her own."

"I wouldn't expect less," Hemlock said. "My Court Magician's safety is vital to the safety of the kingdom. What do you want from me?"

"I want to draw him out," I said. "Are you holding an Affection Day feast?"

"Are you kidding?" she countered, her face alive with scorn. "It's a fake holiday so the merchants can make money. Even if my husband was still alive, I wouldn't put the kingdom in debt for the sake of sentiment."

"Is it worth it to keep your Court Magician and General of the Army happy?"

"Perhaps," Hemlock said, narrowing an eye at me.

"No, Your Majesty," Grimble said. He was a colorless bureaucrat who only elicited pleasure from an increasing bottom line and by thwarting anyone with imagination. "Such a feast would cost a significant amount of money. I can't see any returns from such an outlay." He glared at me. "Are you paying for it?"

I hesitated, long enough to make it look as though I was concerned about the cost.

"I'll split it with you," I said. I knew Aahz would take my hand off at the wrist if I paid for the whole celebration out of petty cash. I didn't want to tell Grimble that M.Y.T.H., Inc. probably had more wealth stashed under the coffee table in our tent in the Bazaar than was in the treasury under the castle in which we stood. He'd twist the queen's arm to make sure that I had to shoulder all expenses. "After all, this is in your interest as well as mine."

Grimble and I stood eye to eye.

"You pay three-quarters."

"Half," I said. "I could drop my share to a flat nothing and walk away, but the outcome would probably involve your Court Magician leaving town. I'd welcome her back to M.Y.T.H., Inc. She *might* help you find a replacement before she went, but I doubt it."

"Grimble!" Hemlock snarled.

"All right, half," Grimble gritted through his teeth, as though I had just asked to cut out his internal organs. A herald, trumpet under his arm, marched in to announce her next visitors. "I want receipts!"

O O O

"Massha?"

I tapped on Massha's door. Then, I recalled my own instructtions. After years of practicing magik, I had developed an excellent visual memory. I pictured the inside of her study: the big easy chairs around the table with the wine carafe, the rank of chests that held her collection of magik items, the high work table covered with scrolls and small pieces of disassembled gizmos. In the middle of that was a tall, black iron candlestick with a fat white candle. I concentrated on it, willing the wick to kindle into flame. I breathed a wisp of power through the door.

There.

The door flew open. Her orange hair looking wilder than before, Massha grabbed my hand and dragged me inside. Aloft, she all but dragged me like the string of a rogue balloon across to the armchairs.

"Well?" she asked.

"Get dressed," I said. "We're going to a party."

O O O

"This is a terrible idea," Massha said. She had traded her harem pants and top for an embroidered brassiere and a long skirt of the floaty material in bright red. The skirt jingled around the waist and hem with dozens of little trinkets. Massha wore rings on every finger, bracelets and anklets and necklaces enough to sink a treasure ship, most of which gave off a hefty magikal buzz.

"It's the only way," I said. While she dressed, I had gone back to Valentinius's shop in Deva and cut a few deals. Three of his helpers, wearing disguise spells to keep the servants and nobles from fleeing to the hills in terror at the sight of Deveels, put up pink, white, and red decorations and laid out tables with loads of inexpensive Affection Day trinkets. Aahz insisted on coming along.

"To protect my investment," was the way he put it. To keep an eye on me, was far more likely. I also brought General Badaxe along, but only with a promise that he obey my instructions.

We joined the Queen on the steps of the castle keep. A crowd of townsfolk hovered at the gates, watching in wonder at the notion of a free party. Queen Hemlock never entertained. The tax funds that weren't spent on necessary kingdom infrastructure went for her expansion plans of the border of the country. Hemlock wore a tightly kirtled red dress with a slit up the front of each thigh all the way to her waist.

Guido was up on the battlements. Nunzio was outside the gates, listening to the people and watching out for Shilldon. With Bunny's permission, I'd reached out to Don Bruce for some of his other Enforcers. Instead of wearing their usual snappy suits, they wore the same tunics and hose to fit in with the locals.

"This is a terrible waste of money," Grimble said, watching the crowd at the gate.

"It's an investment in one of your key personnel," Aahz said. I had left him untransformed. "That's like saying you won't fix the drawbridge because masons cost money."

"The drawbridge won't drink four tuns of wine. Four!"

"Six," I said. "I want to make sure we have plenty. I don't know how long it will take to smoke Shilldon out."

Grimble was aghast. "Six! That's not what we agreed. Take two of them back to the cellars!"

"Too late," I said, cheerfully. "They've already been tapped." I looked at the sky. The sun had sunk to the top of the peaked cylinder of the Magician's Tower. "It's time."

Massha squeezed my hand.

"Hit it, Guido!" Aahz shouted. The huge Enforcer raised his hand to the armored man-at-arms on the battlement.

With a creak of long-suffering wood and metal, the portcullis lifted. All the nobility within a four-hour ride led the way on handsomely caparisoned steeds, but they were quickly surrounded and passed by the hordes of commoners making for the refreshment tables. Guido and the Enforcers, dressed to match the local Klahds, blended in with the visitors, looking for anything suspicious.

"You're on, kid," Aahz said, clapping me hard on the back.

I kicked my heels together, and the little wings lofted me upward. The crowd gasped and pointed. Some of them shrieked in terror, but most of them cheered for me. I held up my hands.

"Welcome to the Affection Day party!" I announced. "Thanks to the generosity of Her Majesty, Queen Hemlock of Possiltum, you're invited to enjoy an evening of revelry, music, and dance."

"And booze!" a man called from the midst of the crowd.

"Find that man and lock him up," Hemlock said, with a bored wave of her hand. The guards pushed past her and into the heart of the throng. The man dropped his foolish grin and tried to get away, but the mob was too thick. He was dragged away by his heels, yelling and protesting. I watched in horror. The rest of the people didn't seem unduly upset. They were used to their queen's capricious temper.

"C'mon, kid!" Aahz growled.

I pulled my wits together. "Let the festivities begin!"

They all cheered again, and headed for the beer kegs, where kitchen servants were pouring mugs of pink Affection Day ale as fast as they could. The band, hired from the Wild Tonsil Inn in Winslow, struck up a fast reel. Girls dragged reluctant men into the open square and began to dance with them. Carny, a disguised Deveel who normally dealt cards in the Even-Odds, a gaming establishment in which I had had a financial interest, drew people into a lover's quiz. Within minutes, he had managed to elicit blushes, indignant shouts, and laughter from his contestants and audience. Everyone seemed to be having a really good time, crowding together and having fun.

Satisfied, I settled back to the floor.

"That's it for me," Hemlock said, hoisting her heavy skirts in both hands. "I don't intend to stand here and watch ugly peasants get plastered on my coin. I'm going inside. If any of the handsome ones drop out of the quiz, bring them to me. Grimble, keep an eye on everything. If anyone breaks anything, bill it to Master Skeeve." She strode away.

"Yes, your majesty," JR Grimble said, bowing and scraping. I had never been so glad to have left a job. I don't know how I put up with working for Hemlock as long as I had.

Massha was tapping her foot to the music. I had to admit, the Winslovak band was good.

"I don't see Shilldon," she said in a low voice. "Or Hugh."

"Hugh's not here," I said, tersely. "I'm here as his proxy."

"Good," Massha said, with a sigh. "I don't want him to get hurt. This looks like it's turning into a nice shindig. Want to dance, Boss?"

"No," I said. "This party's only a subterfuge. Setting it up was the easy part of my assignment. You've got the hardest part. Can you do it?"

She moved from foot to foot, but it wasn't the music making her vacillate.

"Are you sure this is the only way to find Shilldon?"

"Yes. We've got to draw him out, and you're the only bait we have. Are you ready?"

She squared her big shoulders. "I can do it."

I had had Valentinius set up a small table all by itself at one side of the courtyard. It was bespelled with one of Massha's aversion charms so none of the revelers would sit down at it. It had been placed deliberately so it fell into a gloomy shadow between the flickering light of the two nearest torches. With a great heave of her shoulders, she pushed her way past the dancers and musicians, and sat down heavily on one of the two stools. It groaned like a lost soul under her weight, but anything that drew attention to her was good.

She planted one elbow down on the small table.

And sighed.

And dabbed at her eyes with a dainty hanky.

And sighed again.

A server, hastily called into service by Aahz, sped to her side with a frothy-headed mug of Affection Day ale. Some of the pink liquid sloshed onto the tabletop. She ignored the beverage, except to draw little designs in the spill, concentrating on them.

I waited.

A cheer went up from the contest booth, where Carny had just drawn the winners of the first round of the True Confessions game. Massha watched them with an expression of woe. But no one came to sit down beside her. The revelers polished off their first mugs of ale and went back for refills, laughing and joking with one another. Young men and women paired off, then decoupled and found new partners. Where was Shilldon?

"Do you see him yet?" Aahz asked.

"No," I murmured back, scanning the crowd. "But he could be disguised as anything."

"Or nothing," Aahz said, suddenly. "Watch Massha."

I did. She raised her head and looked at me.

No, not at me. Her focus seemed to be much closer to her. Her eyes went wide with shock, and her mouth dropped open. She was frightened! I started toward her. Aahz pulled me back.

"No. Watch."

I yanked my arm loose from his grasp, but I didn't move.

Massha's eyebrows went up, as though listening to a question. The corner of her mouth crooked upward, and she modestly dropped her gaze. Then she looked up toward me again. Her eyes darted from side to side as though studying something intently. Her lips parted slightly. One of her hands went forward and flattened on the table. She smiled.

"So that's how he brought those love notes to her," I said, enlightenment dawning. "He's invisible!"

"That's a tricky piece of magik," Aahz said, with a critical glance. "How much power is he pulling down?"

I opened my mind's eye and looked at the empty stool. Suddenly, I saw a shimmering outline of a large man.

"He's there," I said. "And there's something really strange about him. It doesn't look like a spell. He's not pulling magikal energy from the force lines below the castle."

"Has to be a device of some kind," Aahz said. "A cloak or a ring."

"She's acting as if she can see him," I said. "How can we be looking right through him if she can see his face?"

"That's one sophisticated piece of hardware, whatever it is. I've read about items like that in the catalog from a Pervish manufacturer I know. Doesn't come cheap. He's been planning this for a long time. Massha's in real trouble."

I watched her, helplessly. If I hadn't known better, I would say she was carrying on one half of a flirtation, one that was progressing steadily. She took a stray lock of her lank orange hair between thumb and forefinger and pulled it back over her ear.

"But what can he do? He can't just sweep her out of here."

"No, that's the beauty of it," Aahz said, narrowing his big yellow eyes. "He's convincing her to go with him of her own free will. Look at her face."

Since the Jahk was invisible, I could see right through him, in more ways than one. Even with Hugh Badaxe madly in love with her, Massha had admitted to me she'd never felt really attractive. To have someone who insisted that he couldn't live without her had to be pretty overwhelming. Shilldon made her feel beautiful.

"I'm going over there," I said. "I'm going to tear his cloak off and reveal him to everyone!"

Aahz clamped a scaly hand on my arm and hauled me back again.

"Calm down, kid," he said. "There's no way you can take him. This is a Jahk. He's used to competing—and winning. And if he's about Massha's age, he has twice your experience, and probably a hundred magik items, all of which he's an expert at using. And it looks like he's charming as hell. She was scared out of her mind to meet up with him. Now she's acting like a kitten. That's a powerful personality. What do you have?"

I fumed for a minute on Massha's behalf, then I stopped to think about it. Hard. Then, I smiled.

"I have you."

He grinned, showing all of his four-inch pointed teeth.

"Right. That's not all. You've got special abilities today. You've been sworn in as an Affection Day messenger. What's that suggest to you?"

I clutched the bowstring that stretched from my chest to my hip.

"I can't shoot him! What if he really is Massha's one true love?"

He eyed me.

"And what do you really think the odds of that are? Think! She told you he never went through the Affection Day ritual with her. He said he didn't need to. What's that suggest to you?"

"That he's sure it isn't true," I said. I eyed him, speculating. "Does the arrow really help you identify your real love, or just someone who *could* love you?"

"The effect's temporary," Aahz said, his voice a low, amused purr. "It just adds spice to the relationship. Do you think I'd be sending you out to a dozen honeys if I thought they'd all be coming for me at once?"

I felt my eyebrows rise. Then I reached for my bow.

"I think I have an Affection Day delivery to make."

I marched across the crowded square. The dancing couples waved and smiled at me as I passed.

"Shoot us!" a middle-aged matron cried, crushing one of the disguised Deveels in a passionate embrace. The Deveel looked terrified. "He's marvelous!"

"I'll be back," I said.

Massha glanced up at me as I approached. For just a moment, I saw the outline of a handsome face with a pronounced jaw, then it vanished.

"Skeeve, what are you doing?" she asked.

"Aren't you going to introduce me to your friend?" I asked, pointedly turning to the empty stool. In my mind's eye, I could still see the outline of a body. It was much larger than mine, with shoulders twice as wide and hands the size of my head. I wasn't going to let mere size intimidate me. Massha was counting on me!

"Um, sure," Massha said. Her voice trembled. "Skeeve, this is Shilldon. He's … he's the love of my life."

The face I had glimpsed appeared again. Shilldon wore a self-satisfied smirk. Even though I wanted to punch him out, I was struck by how absurdly handsome he was. I was good at spotting illusions, and this was no illusion. He had wide, chiseled cheekbones, a noble brow, clear green eyes, and a mouth that was at once masculine but soft. By comparison, he made me feel like a scarecrow, and the ridiculous messenger suit didn't do anything to help.

"Nice to meet you, Shilldon," I said. "When are you leaving Klah?"

The smirk broadened.

"As soon as I can convince this gorgeous lady to come with me," he said. His hand appeared on top of Massha's on the table. His fingers squeezed hers tightly—a little too tightly. "I've been searching for her for years."

Massha's mouth smiled, but her eyes screamed *Get me out of this!* I nodded to her reassuringly.

"That's really nice," I said. "But you know she's married."

"So what?"

Now I really wanted to kick him. I kept my tone friendly.

"If you really loved her, you'd pay attention to the way she wants to live. And that's not with you, or wouldn't she have stayed with you?"

"But she's my true love," Shilldon said, turning his handsome face to her. "The one that got away. I want her back. Isn't that right, my darling? You've been waiting for me all this time, sad and lonely?"

Massha melted toward him longingly. Even I was beginning to be affected by his charm. It dawned on me that maybe that was being generated by a magikal gizmo, too.

"What if she doesn't want you?" I asked.

"Of course she does!" he said. He looked deeply into Massha's eyes. "Sweetheart, why don't you throw this skinny pipsqueak over the wall, and we'll go off and live happily ever after?"

Never breaking the intense gaze, my former apprentice flicked her wrist. A huge wave of energy hit me under the chin like an uppercut. I sailed upward toward the courtyard battlements, flying end over end.

I flapped my arms to stop spinning. It took me a moment to get my wits back and used a handful of magik to stop my outward trajectory. I hovered for a moment, working my jaw to make sure it was still intact. That blow had hurt! Shilldon was a master manipulator, getting Massha to attack me instead of doing it himself. That was it! He had to go.

I reversed my course and headed back toward him, under my own power this time.

"Hey, Shilldon," I called. "Happy Affection Day!"

I pulled one of the pink-fledged arrows out of my quiver and nocked it to the bowstring.

Shilldon's green eyes widened in horror. The face rose as if he sprang from his seat. Then he yanked Massha up and held her before him.

"You won't shoot me," he said. "You'll hit Massha!"

The shadow figure I could only see in my mind's eye huddled down behind her. Her broad body made a good shield. I could have moved around to the other side. But I was pretty sure I didn't have to. He wasn't in control of the situation. He'd have to peek out sooner or later to see what I was doing.

Wait for it, I told myself, the sharp string cutting into the joints of my fingers. *Wait for it.... There!*

I loosed. The arrow took Shilldon right between the eyes. He fell backward and measured his whole length on the cobblestones. The shaft of the arrow disappeared, and pink feathers floated down onto his face.

A billowing cloud of nothingness floated off his body, revealing a tall, muscular frame. So it had been a cloak! He tried to sit up, but I hovered over him and peppered him with more arrows.

"Let's find you the *real* love of your life, or at least for tonight!" I said.

On the dance floor, a handful of girls and a few men stopped gyrating and looked around. All at once, they saw Shilldon.

"Oh, my God, he's gorgeous!" a tall redhead shrieked. She abandoned her partner and ran toward Shilldon, her arms out. A black-haired beauty caught up and blocked her way.

"Don't you dare touch him! He's mine!"

"I want him!" a slender man dressed in pink Affection Day garb said, throwing himself at the prone Jahk. "He fell out of nowhere to be with *me*!"

In a moment, more than a dozen people were fighting over Shilldon, tearing at his clothes, covering him with kisses and caresses. He scrambled backward, trying to get away from them.

"Massha, help me!" he cried.

My former apprentice looked down at him. Her jaw set.

"No."

Shilldon looked up at her in shock and disbelief. The mass of loving bodies covered him, hiding him from sight, weighing him down.

Bamf!

The would-be lovers collapsed to the ground. Shilldon was gone.

"He's gone!" the redhead cried, feeling the empty cobblestones in vain.

"How could he leave me?" the black-haired woman wailed.

"You?" the slim man said, consumed by woe. "How could he leave *me*?"

I felt around the ground until I touched the edge of the unseen cloth and gathered it up. Having an invisible cloak might come in handy one of these days.

"Where did you learn to shoot like that, boss?" Massha asked.

"Hunting lizard-birds in the forest before I met Garkin," I said. "If I wasn't good, I didn't eat."

"Well, that was one lizard-bird I'm glad you shot," she said. She glanced around, warily, but Shilldon was nowhere in sight. "I can't believe that I ever thought he was the one. Do you think he'll be back?"

"I doubt it," I said. "He used you as a shield to protect himself. You know now that he's a coward." I pulled an arrow from my quiver. "Are you still afraid that he's the one you're really meant for?"

Massha smiled. "Not anymore. It's Hugh, now and forever." She pulled the sides of her red bodice apart, revealing an expanse of cleavage. "Hit me, boss. I'm ready."

O O O

"Where'd she go?" Aahz asked, as I returned to the side of the dance floor. A serving maid offered him a bucket of pink ale. I dropped my hat on the table and propped my bow against the wall. The gems flashed on and off like lightning bugs, bathing us in pink, red and white light. The servant poured me a mug of beer.

"To the cottage," I said. I took a long drink. My throat was dry. In spite of its bizarre color, the beer tasted pretty good. "Hugh's been waiting there all evening. It almost killed him not to be here, but he's a good general. He knows when to fight his own battles, and when to send out special forces instead. I doubt we'll see them until morning." I worked my jaw with one hand. It still hurt where Massha had struck me. "What a weird festival. No wonder Hemlock never celebrates it."

"Nah," Aahz said, taking a gulp of ale. "This is the best Affection Day I've ever seen."

"Maybe one day I'll have someone special to enjoy it with."

Aahz clapped me hard on the back. "You already did, partner."

"Huh?"

"You saved a friend from an abusive ex-lover. You helped her rekindle her romance, and that was a hot one already. If you can't enjoy that, you're hopeless." He grinned. "And now Hemlock owes us a favor. It was worth the two or three gold pieces we had to kick in to make this work."

"That's right," I said. All of the preparations had really worked out to almost nine gold pieces. I vowed to keep the other receipts out of Aahz's sight when I squared up with Grimble. I stretched out my arms and yawned. "Well, I don't know about you, but I'm exhausted. I think I'll just go back to Deva and get some sleep." I reached for the rest of my beer.

Aahz picked up my hat and set it on my head. He took the mug away from me and shoved the bow into my hand.

"No, you're not," he said. "You've still got a dozen deliveries to make for me before midnight. Get going!"

I tipped my glittering hat.

"Anything for a friend," I said, before I *bamfed* out.

Mardi Gras

Wash Away the Sins

The mellow *clip-clopping* of the horse's hooves on the cobblestone pavement sounded perfect amidst the iron curlicues and multicolored paint of the buildings looming on either side. The driver of the open landau grinned through his thick, neat, blond beard. He wore a suit that harkened back two centuries, but the velvet of the coat was as smooth and pristine as the day it was woven, and the folded cravat shone white at his throat.

"Pride of New Orleans!" he shouted. "Come and see the finest city in North America, bar none! The tou-ah be leavin' from whatever street corner you standin' on. Where y'at? Pride of New Orleans tou-ah! How about you, little lady? You and your friends, fifty dollahs?" He tipped the stem of his whip to the brim of his top hat in a little salute.

The girls in the t-shirts giggled and clutched their plastic Hurricane cups. They shook their heads. Pride gave them a grin and drove on. No need to grab for a few tipsy souls now. The time for the great gathering was later on. The parades had yet to start.

He sniffed the air. His fellow Gluttony was somewhere about. The overwhelming smell of food and drink that saturated the air over the odor of unwashed humans, tobacco, vomit, and mold wasn't due to the restaurateurs and bar owners kicking it into high gear. Gluttony couldn't help but reek of his obsession no matter where he went. Most of the people in the streets were strangers. They didn't realize that the French Quarter didn't usually smell like that. Otherwise they might take warning.

He turned into Rampart and made a quick right down St. Ann's toward Jackson Square. The streets were full of tourists laden with throws and locals in costume. That pleased him. Should be a good day.

The other Manifestations must have thought so, too. He spotted Greed, that skinny minx in her designer jeans and tight camisole, following a couple of teenaged boys from up north as they moved just a little too casually through the elbow-to-elbow crowd past a store along the northeast side of Jackson Square. Her eyes changed from hazel to gold as they snagged a few throws off the nearest display and stuffed them up under their t-shirts. The expensive ones were in plain view of the proprietor, a round-bellied black man in his fifties with his arms crossed over his chest. Greed dropped back, stricken. They weren't up to her standards.

Small stuff, Pride thought haughtily. *Chickens. If they'd been serious about it, distracted the owner, pulled a little fast-talking, they could have had the twenty-dollar necklaces, at a minimum.* He felt sorry for Greed. She had tried, but the material was just not there. He looked at the grand clock at the other end of the square. Its hands had nearly met at the top. Only twelve hours to go, and neither one of them was doing much of a job.

They were not there on their own impulse. The Big Guy had a sense of humor about his most beloved creation, humankind. It pleased Him to send the personifications of the most deadly sins to tempt mortals into a state of disgrace.

The strains of a jazz band struck up in the distance. Pride turned his horse toward Bourbon Street. This was the moment he had been waiting for. If he couldn't snare a few souls who were pride-ridden beyond help on board those floats, then he wasn't much of an absolute. He needed to instill an overweening belief in their own superiority, so they would have something to repent come midnight and Ash Wednesday. Those souls—their souls—

depended upon it. By exaggerating the small sins that everyone carried inside themselves, the Manifestations made it easier to recognize them, rue them, and put them aside for good. They would be washed clean for another year. If they resisted sinning, so much the better for them. An experienced and repentant soul made a better angel than a stifled hermit. If not, the Devil was waiting, and he had gotten a lot more unrepentant souls than he deserved over the last few years. Come life's end, unwary mortals would find themselves in Hell, sunk down by a load of sin they hadn't bothered to get rid of when they had the chance. Pride had been there more than once, and never wanted to go back. The devil himself wasn't a bad fellow—in fact, he was pretty good company, and more honest than any of his unwilling guests—but just like in real estate, it was all about location. Heaven wasn't just about having the good things, but their proximity. Proximity was the reward. In Hell, all those good things were there, but just out of reach: food, water, shelter, comfort, love. Forever. Pride shuddered. Best to keep as many souls as he could from having to suffer the deprivation. He wanted them to get down on their knees and pray on Wednesday for forgiveness, even if their only prayer was, "Dear God, I am so sorry I drank all those Hurricanes. If you take away this hangover, I swear I will never do that again."

Pride's job hadn't been so hard in the past. People he tempted confessed more readily to their sins. He put it down to less enthusiastic church-going and a belief that nothing they did had any consequences. Hurricane Katrina had pushed people back to the congregations in droves once they had lost everything, but they were drifting away again, even though they were still unsatisfied and unfulfilled. It was strange, but humanity felt as if it was dead inside. They came to New Orleans and Mardi Gras to try and feel alive. These were the ones Pride hoped he could reach. He touched his crop to his horse's flank to hurry her up. He didn't want to miss the Rex parade. That was the big one.

Pride drove his beautiful carriage into a nook on Bourbon Street that to mortals looked no larger than a mail slot, and emerged into a sunlit courtyard surrounded by white marble walls and fluted pillars. New Orleans was full of passages into the real world. This was the entrance to his domain. There was room enough for fifty carriages inside, or anything else he wanted stowed there, though he had no need of storage space. His horse dislimned in a burst of brilliant white light, and the carriage dissolved in shadows. He could summon anything he wanted into being, temporarily or permanently, a skill he admitted he was proud of. Over his shoulder, he noticed a twenty-something young man with dark skin who had followed him in. The youth looked at the place where the horse and carriage had stood, then at the glass in his hand, and scrambled back out of the entrance. Pride grinned.

Pride took his place at the top of the parade route so he could see every single float that passed, every band, every dancer. Envy was the one who had started the contest among the Manifestations for each to get as many souls secured as he or she could. Greed and Gluttony had rushed to second the notion. Pride usually won the contest at festivals, because they were usually celebrations of a mortal's affiliations, whether of ethnicity, gender or interest. He and Anger shared the honor at political conventions. That almost made up for Greed's absolute hold on Christmas. He could see her taking her place about half a block down, with a good view of a three-story house with iron railings where shapely female exhibitionists were already flashing their breasts at the crowd. Up and down went the scanty t-shirts, to the delighted roars of men and not a few women and Lust. The big, well-built male Manifestation was red-faced with pleasure. He had a girl in each arm. His hands traveled up and down their bodies, bringing them to writhing, near orgasmic, pleasure. They didn't care who saw them. Lust did a thriving trade in alleyway sex during Mardi Gras as well as the flashers, not to mention the strip clubs and professional hookers who plied their wares in doorways and windows around the Quarter. Pride could already see the glow, invisible to mere humans, that said Lust was having a productive day.

Sloth was somewhere around, accumulating followers of his own. He loved the parade-*goers* because they were there to enjoy themselves by doing the least possible and still have the most fun. The entertainment was there for them to enjoy without having to lift a finger. The weather was good, and you barely had to stretch out a hand to secure a drink, or a bead necklace, or a partner to dance with. Pride felt the easy pleasure of Sloth's influence spread out over the crowd. New Orleans's longtime motto was "Laissez les bon temps roulez," or, translated from the local Franglish, "Let the good times roll."

And roll on they did.

The jazz bands of New Orleans had been legendary, and rightly so. After the hurricane, musicians had been slow to return, but there were plenty of them this year. The lead float of the Rex parade was led by a cadre of horns and woodwinds, all in the hands of old and middle-aged men, most of them African-American, dressed in sherbet-colored satin suits with derby hats to match, dancing and jiving as they progressed along Bourbon.

Behind them came the face of a dragon. It looked fierce and proud, painted in rainbows of color but predominantly the purple, green, and gold of Mardi Gras, and sparkling with rows and swirls of lights that blinked and rolled in rhythm, making the dragon look as if he was dancing to the music. Above the face, the king and queen of Rex, resplendent in white satin and masked in feathers, waved to the crowd from the lofty perch of their float; their court, also gorgeously dressed and arrayed around them also waved. The King of Rex and his consort had been chosen from among their krewe as the supreme embodiment of justice and authority. Their very stance showed how much they enjoyed their position of honor. Pride drank in their self-esteem and fed it back to them in waves.

Live for it, he told them. *Bask in it. You deserve every moment of it. You are better than all of those who worship you.* The king's back straightened, and the queen's long, slender neck seemed to lengthen further. *Good,* Pride thought. *That'll hold you through the day.* He saw them on their way, glowing with ego. His talent worked best on those most receptive to it. Envy couldn't touch them. They were real royalty for this day.

Lust had chosen the same couple as a focus. His hot red energy surrounded and suffused the court. A few of the princesses shifted uncomfortably on their flower-strewn benches. The king and queen eyed one another from behind their masks, their glances promising a dynastically good time later on. Pride grinned.

Greed hopped up and down on her narrow spike heels, beckoning the court to throw beads to her. She and those around her she had charmed were already festooned with enough sparkling throws to break their backs, but they must have more, armloads more. She worked her wiles upon the crowd, until they were shrieking in expectation at the riders on the float, demanding necklaces and doubloons. Pride watched with caution. Another of Envy's contests was to see how many humans they could take away from one another. Pride found it counterproductive and seldom participated in it. Sloth, flabby and proud of it, could rarely be bothered to fight for mortals. He lounged on a second-floor balcony with a host of onlookers who were just enjoying the view. Pride couldn't sense Anger anywhere. Mardi Gras was frequently a disappointment to his red-eyed friend, with so many people getting into the spirit of good times. He was pleased to see that the Rex court was unaffected by Greed. Regally, they tossed rope after shining rope of beads and handfuls of gold coins to her minions, enjoying the pleasure they spread.

The Rex parade ended and was succeeded by Zulu, then Orpheus, Bacchus, Saturn, and a dozen other krewes, all filling Bourbon Street with music and glitter. Pride found willing followers in each one. He was pleased and satisfied with himself. The crowd swelled larger and larger until when the music of the last jazz band faded away, it filled the twilit streets. Gluttony and Lust took over, sending the multitude in search of other forms of satisfaction. Gluttony had found turtle soup and crawfish étouffée somewhere, because the rich, heady aromas filled the air. Greed was for the moment sated, lost under a shining cloak of beads. Sloth lolled on his balcony, waves of laziness rolling out from him.

At nightfall, Pride left them to their pleasures. Wearing an impeccable evening suit and a purple mask he had picked up in sixteenth century Venice, he slipped into the first of the elegant balls, at the Art Museum. Exclusivity drew him. The people who were privileged to pass through the doors, past the *hoi polloi*, were already prideful. He fed their egos, giving them a sense that they were more worthy, more exalted, and just plain better than the man on the street. No matter that in their normal lives they were plumbers and store clerks; tonight they were the elite, with over a hundred years of history behind them. He sailed into masquerades, dinners, dances, and discos, buoying the pride that each man and woman had in themselves and the spirit of the day.

Envy's mortals hung around the doors of the same hotels, wishing with all their hearts that they could pass through those portals and into the exalted enclaves, resenting those who could. Pride patted Envy on the shoulder as he went by. She shot him such a look of hate that he felt pity for her.

In the Orpheus party, masked dancers filled the room, but the walls were lined with tables manned by catering staff dressed in waistcoats and white gloves. They helped the guests to an opulent buffet of food and drink ranging from jambalaya to beignets, champagne to whisky. Gluttony, a plate in each hand and one balanced on each arm, gave him a nod from behind a gold pig's mask. Pride sampled a taste of each dish, bestowed well-deserved compliments and energy upon the caterers, and departed for the next party. He crossed paths with all of his companions at one party or another. Greed danced with a wealthy man wearing huge diamond cufflinks on his ruffled French cuffs. She wore a priceless gold necklace taken from a dead king of Persia over eight centuries before. Each coveted the other's treasure. Pride could see they were blissfully happy.

Lust was in the corner of every ballroom, whispering suggestions into the ears of masked couples who stole moments away from their mates or chaperones. Sloth lolled at his leisure on couches surrounded by those who had eaten, drunk or danced their fill and didn't want to bestir themselves further. Envy appeared at the shoulder of servers who waited upon the honored guests but were never part of the party. She, too, was amassing followers within doors as well as without.

To Pride's surprise and relief, Anger was absent from any of the events he attended. Everyone was being well-behaved and temperate. With so much alcohol and stimulation, it was … unnatural. Anger could not have ignored the divine summons to service there in New

Orleans, nor would he lack adherents. The streets were full of drunks spoiling for a fight after Gluttony filled them with liquid courage. Midnight would strike soon, when the holy time of Ash Wednesday descended, offering peace and salvation to those who embraced the divine strictures of self-denial and penance.

Then he felt it. The sensation was so strong he did not understand how he had missed it. Red-brown waves of fury and hatred washed into the room, so that even couples paired by Lust stopped to look at one another in suspicion. Pride was beside himself with outrage. Anger had no right to ruin events for him!

Time and distance were no barriers to communication with his fellow Manifestations.

"Anger!" he demanded, knowing his voice would reach the other's ears. "Stop it at once!"

"I can't!" Anger growled. "Come out and help me!"

Pride was so astonished that he didn't make a sour comment about the other's attack of humility. He rushed out of the ball. As he passed Greed, he took her by the arm.

"I almost had those diamonds," she complained.

"Anger needs us. He is outside."

Greed's mouth dropped open with shock. Abandoning her quarry, she undulated toward the buffet table and removed Gluttony from his leisurely perusal of the dessert trays.

"Enough!" she commanded. "Go find Sloth. We need him."

"Oh, have pity!" he wailed. "I need my nourishment before it's too late. Midnight is striking."

Indeed it was, Pride remarked. Bells in church towers all over the city began to peal, a cascade of commanding tones to the revelers to give up their earthly pleasures, in anticipation and certain hope of the heavenly treasures that would await them. Pride rushed out of the door of the hotel, into a shouting crowd. A couple of men were fighting in the street, with the others egging them on. Police on horseback were advancing on them, the water cannons that cleared detritus off the pavement in their wake. The men paid no attention. But a lone fistfight wasn't enough to cause despair in one of the seven deadly Sins.

Pride spotted Envy in the crowd.

"Where is Anger?" he asked.

"I don't know," she said. "He feels as if he is everywhere."

It did feel as if the entire city was filled with rage. The water cannons blew the garbage to the gutters, but to Pride's amazement, they could not knock over the two men brawling. He had never seen such a thing before. Their anger kept them upright against the torrent. When police moved in to try and remove them, the men pulled them down out of their saddles and began to attack them. The police struggled to their feet, ankle deep in water, and started pounding their aggressors.

The last chime of midnight rolled, and the sky fell silent. Pride waited. The fight should stop now. Anger's influence should fade, as would each of the other Manifestations, but it didn't. More people waded into the battle, some to rescue the police and some to defend the original combatants.

Anger was not there, but his influence overspread the city. Pride turned his back on the fight and headed toward the strongest feeling of fury. It came from the direction of the riverfront. Gesturing to the others to follow, he pursued it. Once Pride crossed Chartres into Jackson Square, he found the center of the emotional maelstrom. A crowd of thousands of people, all punching and pushing one another, jammed the grassy square at the center, thronged the cobblestoned streets, and threw one another up against the gracious buildings that ringed them. Every color, male and female, straight and gay, striking out in every direction, their voices raised in absolute fury.

"You ran away when the hurricane hit!" an old black woman shouted at a uniformed policeman, striking him in the chest with a bony forefinger. "I was stuck in my attic for three days!"

"The drug lords took over!" he bellowed back. "They shot at us. They shot at our goddamned *helicopter*. We were trying to help save you! No one helped us."

A burly white man in jeans and a plaid shirt pushed between them. "We wanted to help! We drove for hours to be here. We brought our goddamned fire truck and all our medical supplies. *Our town* needed it, but we came here! And a hell of a lot of thanks we got."

The old woman took him on as well. "You think we wanted to stay? They shut us in the stupid, cursed Superdome that fell apart over our heads. You said you would shoot us if we crossed the bridge."

A slender man in tight jeans and an open lame shirt regarded them all with rage. "Aren't you ever gonna get over the damned hurricane? *We've* all moved on!"

A black teenager took him by the shoulder and spun him around. "How dare you think we can just move on? Like it didn't never happen? We live here!"

"So what? That gives you any special privileges?" More people got into the argument.

"What do you out-of-towners think you're doing, coming in here and pissing on our streets? Do you think we're some kinda frickin' Disney World? You throw you hurricane cups all over the place and you insult our women? This is our heritage!"

"You call this a real town? This *is* an amusement park!"

"You all ate up all kinds of resources, and you don't even get jobs!"

"You think we don't want jobs? We want jobs and decent houses, and you want us to leave half our city as empty lots when we have a housing shortage?"

And from every one of them, a challenge to the others who faced them: "Who the hell do you think *you* are?"

Pent up anger rolled out in waves. Untapped oceans of hatred and fear and resentment had been boiling beneath the surface here for years. Pride had not even suspected it. He withdrew his influence wherever he could, so the combatants weren't acting out of mere ego, but it didn't dampen a single temper. He had to find Anger.

He was in the middle of a huge crowd brawling in the middle of the square. Police on horseback were trying to drive them away, but they were not backing down.

"Anger!" Pride shouted. "Stop! Midnight has struck!"

Anger's eyes were glowing red. He stood with fists clenched, as though he was unaware of the mayhem around him. Pride tried to reach him, but Anger was concentrating too deeply.

"Someone wake him up," he ordered.

Lust, Gluttony, Envy and Greed looked at once another.

"Oh, hell's doormat, all right," said Sloth. A wave of relaxation flowed out of the tubby form, causing fighting humans all around them to drop their fists and back away, panting. Anger's eyes faded to their normal russet color.

"What took you so long?"

Pride drew himself up haughtily and glared.

"What did you do?" he demanded. "You're ruining Mardi Gras! These mortals were supposed to have one final, joyful evening then spend tomorrow on their knees, for their souls' sake! It should have started already!" He pointed at the clock, which showed ten past midnight.

"*I* want them on their knees," Lust said, grinning ferally.

"Shut up," said Envy. Pride knew how hard it was for her to find a mate. She was never satisfied with the ones she found, always feeling that someone better was not far away.

"This is a powder keg," Anger said, and Pride could tell that, perversely, he was enjoying it. "These people are almost more furious than they were in the race riots in Los Angeles. Or the Taiwanese parliament! Or the French Revolution!" He leered with pleasure.

Pride smacked him across the face. Anger gaped. "Snap out of it! This is out of control. It will *become* the French Revolution in a while. What happens when all the parties in the hotels and pubs end and the riverboats dock, and the guests try to go home? Through this? Bring it to an end! You know the laws. Divine retribution will follow, not only for these mortals, but for us! We will cease to exist in this place. We don't belong here any longer. Can you see what is building here? Can you hear them?" Pride exclaimed. "They'll burn this city to the ground. They deserve better than another disaster. Let their emotions return to normal levels."

Envy was scornful. "Deserve? Since when does *deserve* lead to *get*?"

"Always!" screeched Greed. "Always!"

Pride sighed. The problem with Sins was that each of them had their own agenda. He always held himself as their unofficial leader, but that hierarchy could be turned in a moment. Anger was poised to take command from him.

"It will fade," Anger said, but he looked uncertain. "It is fading."

A wild scream interrupted them. Men near them sprang apart as a body in their midst fell to the ground. A knife was planted in its chest. Blood bubbled from the terrible wound. The victim gasped vainly for his life. Police clubbed their way through to the scene of the murder. More fights were breaking out over whose fault it was. Pride set his lips in a grim cast.

"End it. End it now. Dawn is coming."

"Don't lecture me!"

"They're your followers. You're responsible for them. And you asked for our help."

Anger glared at him, but nodded. He closed his eyes and concentrated. Pride could sense it as the Manifestation withdrew his influence. His own temper cooled to its ordinary placid dignity. He looked around, waiting for calm to overtake the crowd.

It didn't. The fighting raged on with the same intensity. The Manifestations were surrounded by faces running with blood, and more pointless arguments erupted. A loud crash sounded from the end of the square, and Greed let out a shriek.

"They are destroying the stores! They aren't stealing, they are ruining! What a waste of all those goodies! Stop them, stop them!"

"I can't," Anger said, his teeth gritted.

"They want what they can't have," Envy said. "Peace of mind. We are superfluous to them now. They enter the new day with no repentance. They will all be damned!"

"Forget damned, they're hurting each other," Sloth said. "What happened to letting the good times roll?"

"Is that all you ever think about, you lazy galoot?" asked Lust.

"Of course. What else?"

Anger turned to Pride. "What should we do?"

"Can we distract them? Put their minds on something else? Will that break the rage?"

Anger nodded, his hot brown eyes burning as he listened to the hearts of his followers. "It should."

"Circle around him," he ordered the others. Envy glared, but obeyed. The six joined hands and concentrated on spreading their own influence. Pride reached out to the adherents he could sense in the growing throng. They must consider their own dignity now, he told them. "You are too far above this to resort to name-calling and assault. Draw back. Return to your homes. Maintain calm and set an example."

Across the square, those in whom pride was the strongest dropped their fists and backed away from their opponents. If their rivals were surprised, it added to the feeling of the prideful ones that they were making the best decision. They started to withdraw.

Then Envy's aura touched his, infiltrated it. The humans in Pride's cadre felt their self-esteem grow, but they began to doubt whether they were as well regarded as they felt they ought to be. No one should stand above them! Anger reasserted itself, in spite of the Manifestation's inaction. Fights were rejoined. A large, heavy African-American immediately ahead of him drew his arm back and socked his opponent, an equally hefty white man. The second man fell, working his jaw.

Pride broke out of his trance and dropped Envy's hand. "Stop broadcasting," he said. "You're making things worse."

Envy was instantly offended.

"Do you think I'm not equal to the rest of you?" she demanded.

Pride put his arm around her shoulders. He would have to deal with her later, but not now, not when so many mortals were at risk. "You are the epitome, the absolute of your emotion," he said gently. "But you are too effective. No one can withstand your influence. You're adding to their sense of resentment."

"That's what I do!"

"But not now," he pleaded. "It's after midnight. Dawn is coming."

"Don't you dare single me out!" she shrieked. "You're saying I'm not as good as you are!"

"I'm not," Pride said. Even if he felt it was the truth, now was not the time to say so. "Just be still for the moment."

Angrily, Envy tugged her other hand out of Sloth's and stood beside Anger in the center. "Just get it over with. We'll deal with this later."

Pride nodded. He reached out to his followers again. He brought his influence to bear on as many of his adherents as he could touch. To his horror, the brimming well of anger was so powerful that it overwhelmed the mortals' good sense. Instead of backing down, they redoubled their efforts to conquer their opponents. A regal-looking gentleman in evening dress who had been about to back away from a dancer from the Gay Pride krewe suddenly advanced upon him and began to poke the man in the chest, hammering home every syllable of his argument. The dancer did a spin on one foot and delivered a roundhouse kick to the well-dressed man's jaw. He toppled over backwards and measured his length on the cobblestones. As soon as he could regain his feet, he grabbed the dancer by the shoulders and head-butted him.

No! Pride thought at them. *That's not what you should be doing.* But it was his own fault. He glanced at Envy. She was going to crow, but he had no choice. For the sake of the mortals, he had to sacrifice his own pride. He dropped the hands of the Manifestations to either side and stepped into the center of the circle. Anger stared at him.

"Are you giving up on us now?" he demanded.

"No," Pride said, consumed with shame. "I was making things worse. I must stop. Now they feel *justified* in their outbursts of anger."

"So must I," Greed said, coming to stand beside him. "My people are all breaking shop windows."

"You want the three of us to do it all on our own?" whined Sloth.

"Why not? You should be proud of your ability," Pride said, turning all the force of his talent on his companions. The three glanced at one another.

"Come on," Lust said, throwing an arm over Sloth's shoulders. "You, me, and Gluttony? It'll be like old times. Remember all those Roman orgies? It'll be fun."

"Well …" Sloth hesitated. Pride gave every erg of energy he had in him. Sloth shrugged a quarter of an inch. "All right."

It *was* almost fun to watch. To Pride's chagrin, it worked all too well. A man and a woman who had been slapping one another across the face moved closer and closer into a passionate kiss as they were overtaken by a wave of red heat from Lust. Gluttony caused fragrant waves of steam to travel north along St. Peter and St. Ann Streets from the Café du Monde, the aroma of beignets and chicory coffee all but hooking themselves into the noses of half the people in the square. They forgot all about their arguments and wandered away in search of fried dough smothered in powdered sugar. Sloth overwhelmed hundreds of his followers with endless waves of ennui. They simply stopped fighting and sat down on the grass, too exhausted or lazy to continue. Half of them fell asleep where they landed. One by one, the revelers departed.

"Is that all of them?" Pride asked.

"Yes," Greed said, surveying around them. From elbow-to-elbow crowds, the big park seemed almost empty. They sensed beyond the square throughout the city. Every single mortal who hadn't gone home to bed was either eating, drinking, or carousing. To his great relief, the ennui that had stifled the souls of the humans during the day had fled. These people felt alive again. No more emptiness.

"Success," Pride said, smugly. Envy gave him a look of utter disdain.

Behind the Manifestations, the chimes of the church clock tolled a single time. One o'clock.

"We're here too late," Sloth yawned. "Are we gonna get in trouble for running over time?"

"Doubt it," Anger said, with dark humor. "If the Big Guy wants to make everyone sin without us He's going to have to come here in person."

"It's not fair that He loves mortals more than us," Envy complained.

"Watch it!" Pride said. "That kind of comment IS going to get us in trouble."

"What more?" she asked. "I was shut out of every party in town. You treat me like a lesser talent, and kudos go to the self-indulgent sensation hounds in our number. Four of us end up with *no* followers. It's been a horrible day. What else could happen?"

A torrent of water hit her suddenly in the face. The water cannons had finished their work on the side streets and arrived in Jackson Square. All the Manifestations were soaked to the skin before they could vanish into the nearest portal to the real world. Pride's beautiful suit was dripping, and his tie had been knocked askew. Greed was laughing.

"Did I mention the Big Guy has a wry sense of humor?" Pride asked.

After Midnight

Closer. Just a little bit closer. Irmani Sim leaned forward in the polished wooden pew, folding her hands in the lap of her slim-fitting, green satin dress, trying to look as if she was praying. If only that fat man in the shiny blue suit didn't look back at that moment, she'd be in the money—literally. As the minister called out the next hymn, the fat man stood up with the rest of the congregation. He was missing his wallet now, but with any luck, he wouldn't even notice until he tried to pay for breakfast somewhere. Irmani dropped the worn leather billfold into the green crocodile handbag between her feet. Her partner Gib gave her a silly, lopsided grin, teeth shining in his good-looking, dark-skinned face.

"You're going to Hell for that. Stealing in the house of God. Before His very face!" a wispy voice hissed.

Irmani looked around. A stern, wrinkled face like a piece of wadded up newspaper glared at her. The old woman had to be at least ninety, but sharp as broken glass. Irmani frowned. She thought she hadn't been observed. Never mind. She crossed her forefinger over her thumb and pointed it at her accuser.

"You didn't see anything," she whispered. The old woman's face crumpled with confusion for a moment. When it cleared, she smiled a little vacantly at Irmani, then went back to her prayer book.

Irmani and Gib exchanged the kiss of peace with the rest of the congregation and headed back to their seedy little hotel to change out of their Sunday best.

"How much you get?" Gib asked, handing over the two wallets he had lifted during the service.

"Just four," Irmani said, counting twenties with that inward thrill that she always got at the sight of money. "But the pickings will be good this afternoon, I promise. The city is just full of tourists!"

O O O

"Hey, sorry, babe," a tall, fair-skinned man said, clutching her arm with an unsteady hand. His eyes were bloodshot, the result of drinking all the Hurricanes that had been in the stack of cups he carried in his other hand.

"No, it's all my fault," Irmani assured him, putting a friendly hand on his shoulder. Gib nudged up behind him and lifted the wallet out of his pocket and that of the equally drunken friend who swayed and giggled beside him. "Hey, you all have a nice day, huh?"

"We are, babe, we are!" At her mental nudge, they noticed another booth selling Hurricanes on the street and staggered toward it, holding out their towers of glasses. Too bad they weren't going to be able to afford another one unless they left their ATM cards back at their hotel.

With its ornamental painted tiles and fancy curlicue ironwork, the 300-year old French Quarter looked dressed up for Mardi Gras already. There was magic all around the place. Irmani felt it and loved it. Her own talents were shallow by comparison. The Jedi mind trick she pulled on the old lady in the church and the two drunken frat boys were about all she could do, but she was aware of the strong underpinnings of magic in the old city around her. Music was both a part of it and a result of it. She knew little about New Orleans before she got there, but Gib had insisted it would be fun to go to Mardi Gras, so they went.

Irmani laughed at the girls who stood on the antique balconies and yanked up their shirts for strings of beads thrown up to them by shouting men down on the street. There was no way she'd make a public fool of herself for anything, particularly not plastic beads. She noticed that it was only the tourists who did it, not the locals. In fact, she noticed the locals watching her with suspicious eyes from the doorways of residences and shops as she went by, as if they could see the growing stash of purses and wallets in her tote bag. Did they know she wasn't the innocent shopper she appeared to be?

New Orleans was a strait-laced town, much more than she had expected from the come-as-you-are, anything-goes travel brochures. Sure, it was still more than half messed up since the hurricane, but it still had the feel of a place that knew its own mind. It was definitely a Catholic city, like Boston, where she'd spent one miserable week the summer before, but this had a real mind to it, like none of the others had. New Orleans possessed character. It didn't really approve of all those drunk, happy people with money in their pockets, buying round after round of Hurricanes, collecting throws and hot sauce and t-shirts and masks, paying no attention to the condition of wallets or purses, or of her and Gib, either, but it behaved kind of like a maiden auntie. It would let them go on making their own mistakes. It was perfect for her. Irmani had already cleaned up enough to pay for her expenses and still pay rent for two months. What with the Mardi Gras festivities cranking up to full, she might be able to get enough money so her basics were covered for the rest of the year. It'd be nice to take time off. Easier on the nerves.

She and Gib followed the happy crowd down Bourbon Street, around the corner down St. Ann, into Jackson Square. The people were as jammed together and as colorful as jelly beans in a jar. Irmani nodded approval to Gib. This was a good place to start dropping the wallets that they had already emptied of cash. She could count on the press of people to ensure no one could tell who had lost them, just as she could count on human nature to ensure that most of what she dropped would be carried off by someone else who would never think of picking a pocket but would crow over their good fortune and someone else's bad luck. Served them right if theirs was the next billfold to fall into her grasp.

Irmani jumped as she caught two gigantic blue eyes gazing at her. Forcing her heart to slow down, she saw that they were in the massive face of a jester in gold, green, and purple motley that loomed over the heads of the crowd. It was part of a parade float, parked in front of one of the 19th century buildings on the square. If anything, the press of humanity was thicker around it than anywhere else.

"What's going on there?" Gib asked.

"Don't know," Irmani said. "Sounds like opportunity knocking to me!"

"Hear ye! Hear ye! Welcome to all the good subjects of Comus, King of Mardi Gras!" A thin-faced white man in a very fine gray-striped suit stood on a dais just inside the entrance to the Presbytère.

"Be of good cheer! Welcome to all revelers! I am pleased to introduce to you the king and queen of the oldest krewe in all of New Orleans, Comus and his queen!"

He stood aside, clapping his hands. Up onto the dais stepped two of the most fantastic costumes that Irmani had ever seen. She didn't care about the people wearing them, but the outfits had life of their own. Acres of white silk satin had been sewn with thousands of pearls, rhinestones, and sequins into patterns like lace. Velvet cloaks swung from their shoulders, clasped with bejeweled knobs of gold that Irmani swore even from the back of the room were real, as were the necklaces, tiaras, bracelets, and rings. The glorious painted masks that covered the upper part of their faces weren't leather or plastic. Could they be ivory? So much wealth in one place took her breath away. A heavy hand dropped on her shoulder.

"Easy, girl," Gib whispered. "Not for you."

"I know it," she whispered back, peevishly. It didn't do any harm to dream.

The king was speaking. "… As of the earliest members of our sacred order, we want to enrich our mutual heritage. As a token, we are bestowing upon the Presbytère and the Louisiana State Museum these fine artifacts that, according to the documents we have recently discovered, were worn by my many-times predecessor and that of his queen in 1902." He patted the top of a glass display case that was just visible at his left hand. "That makes these older by eight years than the *parure* already on display here. I hope you will enjoy them and the spirit of Mardi Gras. *Laissez les bon temps roulez!*"

Irmani waited impatiently in the long line.

"This had better be worth it," she said to Gib for the nineteenth time. There was no opportunity to increase their personal wealth in the meantime. Gib had pointed out the security cameras aimed down at them from six different spots on the ceiling. She might have been able to fool the minds of the guards, but video tape was out of her reach.

The line took them through a forest of gorgeous costumes. Each was arranged on a life-sized mannequin that wore a wig and a mask. Looking into the empty eye holes gave Irmani the creeps, so she concentrated on the dresses and tunics, and read the posters on the walls.

Properly speaking, the big party going on outside was Carnival. Mardi Gras was only one day, the last blowout. Fat Tuesday, the last day of Carnival, preceded Ash Wednesday, the first day of Lent. Irmani had childhood memories of meatless days and fish on Fridays.

"Did you ever have to give stuff up for Lent?" Gib asked, as if reading her mind.

"Never paid much attention to it, except when I was in Catholic school," Irmani said, dismissively. "The nuns made us do it. We never had to give up anything necessary, only pleasures and vanities, but it was hard. I hated it."

"We had to write ours down," Gib said. "I made it up most times, but my mom wouldn't make dessert all the way through Lent. I mean, is it really giving anything up if you don't get to make the choice? It's supposed to be free will, giving up stuff for God."

"He doesn't care," Irmani said. "If He did, would He have blown this place up with a hurricane?"

Gib shrugged his shoulders.

Finally, it was their turn to pass by the glass case. On a lining of folded purple velvet was a collection of jewelry, the *parure*, as the King of Comus said. The tiara intimidated her, with its rose-cut diamonds, and the ivory domino on a lorgnette was too fussy for her taste, but she couldn't stop looking at the strings of filigree gold beads interspersed with colored gemstones. She knew at once that they were the real thing. Fantastic. She felt her fingers curling into her tingling palms.

"I gotta have that," Irmani breathed.

"Uh-uh," Gib said. "We don't take anything but money. Just money. We don't want anything that hard to fence."

"I don't want to fence them," Irmani said. "I just want them. They are gorgeous!"

"You don't need them, baby," Gib argued. "Look how many throws you've got! Dozens!"

"But they aren't real," Irmani said. "*These* are real."

Gib knew there was no arguing with her once she'd made a decision. The two of them went back out into Jackson Square for the afternoon. Irmani had to drag her mind back over and over so as not to get caught when they did a little business among the steadily increasing crowd.

Just before closing time at five o'clock, they wandered casually in, as if for the first time. Irmani followed the man in the suit, the curator. She sidled up as he was about to lock the cases and gave him a mind-blowing smile. He returned it a little uncertainly, then went back to his task, never realizing there was a gap in his memory as to how many items were in the display after the pretty girl with *café au lait* skin had gone away.

Irmani grabbed Gib, who was hanging out among the mannequins, and dragged him out to the street.

"I got them," she gasped, pulling him around the ironwork fence that blocked off the looming façade of the Presbytère from her sight. Leaning into the branches and leaves that poked through and provided a natural screen, she picked three strands out of the thick rope of sparkling beads that hung around her neck. Gib gawked.

"Look at them," she said. Her eyes, her brain, and heart, felt as if they were filling up with the energy from the glowing jewels interspersed between gold beads. Amethysts, emeralds, and rubies, like pieces of a stained glass window twinkled in her fingers, more real than anything around them.

"We're gonna get in big trouble," Gib said. "Someone's gonna see them."

"So, what if they do? Watch." When she let them go, they disappeared into the jungle of plastic, metal-toned strands, blending in with the cut facets like tigers lurking amid hanging vines. "These are the most perfect things I have ever seen!"

"I dunno, someone must have seen."

"No one did," she said confidently.

"Well, God saw," he said. "I mean, there's a cathedral right there!"

"Oh, come on!" She leaned up and gave him a kiss. "Forget about it. Let's do a little more work, then we can party. We deserve it."

Maybe Gib was right. It was hard to ignore God in New Orleans. God was as omnipresent as the drunks and the mold. She had never been anywhere with so many churches, and everything named Saint this or Saint that. She started to feel eyes on her, but most of them belonged to Blue Dog. She was creeped out by the ever-present paintings of Blue Dogs, whose haunted eyes followed her from numerous shop windows like a bad conscience. She tried not to let them bother her. They were there to have some fun, and to make some serious money.

She consoled herself with the fact that they weren't the only professionals working that crowd. She all but stepped on a tiny woman with wrinkled tan skin in a headscarf who daubed passersby with mustard or hot sauce. When one of her victims turned to exclaim over the "accident," her confederate, a husky young man with straight black hair and black eyes, would loom up and relieve the unlucky tourist of wallet or purse. The little woman apologized over and over in a lilting accent, while the man melted back into the crowd. Irmani had crossed paths with people like them before. They were South Americans. She tried to stay away from them. They didn't like anyone else on their claimed turf.

"Let's just party tonight, huh, baby?" Gib asked, after he had dumped the last few empty billfolds in the men's room of the Café du Monde on Monday night.

"Why not?" Irmani said. She felt full of good will toward her fellow beings. She kept the Comus jewelry around her neck, camouflaged underneath a dozen or so cheap strands. It made her feel precious and special to have them there.

They jammed themselves into the crowd along Bourbon Street to watch a parade. Everyone screamed and laughed with excitement as each float loomed up in the dimness. Faces the size of a car smiled or menaced the revelers. Every parade had its own theme, kept a deep, dark secret until the day of the parade. This one, sponsored by the Mistick Krewe of Bacchus, was the Seven Deadly Sins. The girls on board "Lust" were fully clad, but wearing such sexy costumes that Gib nearly got run over leaning out into the street to stare at them. They laughed at him and threw tons of beads at him. Sheepishly, he gathered them up and gave them to Irmani, just in time for "Greed" to roll into view. Irmani grinned up at the costumed men tossing beads. They rewarded her smile with dozens of fancy beads. She gathered up handfuls. Greed had always been her patron saint.

Now that they were off duty, as she considered it, the two of them joined the throng dancing and laughing along Bourbon Street. The noise was so loud that it felt solid enough to walk on. She let it carry her. The masked and costumed figures on the floats threw her more and more beads. She danced with Gib to the raucous jazz played by live musicians on the floats, banging out of loudspeakers, and blaring out of the doors of the clubs all along the parade route.

"I never want this to end," she said, whirling Gib in a circle until the beads rattled like falling rain. "This is the best time of my life."

But end it always did.

On Mardi Gras Tuesday itself, the tourists began partying early, knowing it was their last chance. Irmani and Gib lifted a few wallets, and noticed they were thinner than the ones they had picked up over the weekend. Everyone was close to having spent all their holiday cash. That was okay. The two of them were done after that night. They could go home and pay off their outstanding bills, maybe get ahead a little bit while Gib looked for a job and she went back to college.

The church bells began to chime. Irmani looked up from her drink as the bonging drowned out the blasting zydeco music in the bar where she and Gib were drinking. The bands put down their instruments. Lights went out all up and down the street. Midnight. Mardi Gras was over. Lent had begun.

She knew better than to go out on the street. Police on horseback herded the crowds off Bourbon Street. For the ones who didn't get the hint, they were blasted off the pavement by the water cannons that followed a few minutes later to clear up the fallen detritus. Irmani watched a cluster of purple, gold and green throws glitter as it turned helplessly in the flow. It was swept away. She lost sight of it by the time it passed the first streetlight.

"All gone," she said, toasting the street with her glass. "Empty. Gone. What fills this place up when Mardi Gras is over?"

"God, maybe," Gib said, solemnly.

"Will you stop saying that?" she asked.

They put money down and staggered out of the bar. The bartender and his busboy looked as though they were glad to see everyone go. Irmani took a deep breath and marched resolutely up Bourbon.

"Where are you going?" Gib asked, catching up with her. He spun her around. "Hotel's this way.

"Right."

Irmani felt an overwhelming urge to go the other way, but Gib was right. She fought the urge. Something had its hand on her shoulder. It kept trying to get her to turn back, like an uncle steering her back to the shop where she'd stolen candy.

She had trouble sleeping. Even though she had some of it underneath her pillow, she spent the night dreaming of the rest of the Comus treasure. She didn't want it, but couldn't stop thinking about it. She mentioned it to Gib the next morning over café latte.

"Gotta give it up for Lent," Gib said, then giggled uncomfortably.

Irmani touched the gorgeous necklaces that lay hidden underneath her zipped up jacket. "No way. They're mine."

"It's vanity."

"I don't care."

Irmani couldn't wear the gorgeous necklaces outwardly any more. Mardi Gras was over. There were still throws and masks for sale in the stores, but only a few tourists bought anything. The festival was over. Everything was dead, warn out, done. The gaiety had gone like a balloon that had been popped. Until the pin hit it at the stroke of midnight it was gorgeous. Now it was a sad rag of rubber that people couldn't wait to throw away. She wanted to get that feeling back, but it just wasn't there to get. Now she knew why blues music made her sad. It expressed the longing for something you desperately wanted and couldn't have.

As they wandered around, she started to notice people on the street with a dab of black on their foreheads. They'd been to church for Ash Wednesday mass.

"Well, they're buying into the superstition," she declared.

Gib looked shocked. So, she admitted, was her twelve-year-old soul, who had gone through confirmation and first communion.

But nothing had ever stopped her from doing what she wanted, so where was God, really?

They didn't have to leave until late that evening. Irmani decided that even if the pickings were slim she might as well do a little business before they went. She and Gib staked out a tourist who still had that air of prosperity. He came out of a shop with a bag full of hot sauce and t-shirts, tucking his wallet back into his hip pocket. Irmani got up close behind him. When he stopped to look into a shop window, she edged nearer as if she was admiring the same display.

A hard hand grabbed her wrist and twisted it up. She cried out and dropped the wallet.

"I'm gonna call the police in just one minute," said the big, dark-skinned man to the shocked tourist. "You pick that up and tell me if anything's missing."

"I didn't do anything," Irmani said, pushing the Jedi mind trick with all the force she could muster. "It's all a mistake. I was handing it back to him."

The tourist looked bemused, then grateful. "That's nice of you, miss."

The bouncer didn't look so sure, but he could no longer remember why he was holding on to her. He let go. Irmani backed away and hurried off. She thought he was still staring after her suspiciously as she walked away.

"Let's get some lunch," Gib said, soothingly. He knew how she hated it when she blew a grab.

Nothing went just right. The steak she got with her grits grillade at lunch was solid gristle, and so was the second one the tut-tutting waitress brought to replace it. She gagged down just enough food to keep her stomach from twisting with hunger.

Irmani couldn't get past the feeling that eyes were on her. Not only the Blue Dog's annoying gaze, but everybody. She used her mind trick on the ones she could see, flinging the charm right and left so they would look away and not see her any more.

"I can't stand it, Gib," she said.

"This town don't want us anymore," he said. "We gotta leave. Our flight's at eight, but we can sit in the airport for a few hours."

There was nothing left in the hotel room that they wanted, and they had been planning to skip out on the bill anyway, so they hailed a taxi on Royal.

"Airport," Gib said.

"Sure thing," the driver said. He was an elderly African-American with a pale, gray-taupe complexion. "You be there before you know it."

It seemed like every billboard they went by had a face on it. The eyes reproached her. She glanced under her jacket at her prized necklaces. They stared at her, too. Every bead had turned into an eye, but not human ones. Angel eyes. Or maybe God's eyes.

They crossed over Rampart heading northward. Irmani felt a lurch, as though all her guts had been yanked out of her body. She leaned back, moaning. She couldn't even close her eyes. When she did, she saw masks. Not even the colorful dominos with the curlicues and the feathers. Just the eyeholes. Empty eyeholes, swallowing her up, swallowing her soul. One mask in particular haunted her: the ivory domino from the glass case in the Presbytère. It reproached her. She was a thief. She didn't need those necklaces to live. They weren't hers. They belonged to Mardi Gras, and Mardi Gras was over. She couldn't do her mind trick on the mask, because it wasn't human. It was speaking for the unseen spirit that was New Orleans.

"What's the matter, honey?" the taxi driver asked, his brown eyes on her from the rear view mirror. "You need me to pull over?"

She nodded, unable to speak. He jerked the car to the curb, waving the vehicles behind him to go around. All the other drivers looked at her as she staggered out and threw up in the gutter. She knew what they were all thinking, as they pierced her with their eyes: a tourist who had had too much partying, but that wasn't it. The driver and Gib each took one of her arms and helped her to sit on the curb.

"Maybe you should give it a day, honey," the driver said, sympathetically, patting her arm. "They won't let you on the jet like that. Go on back. Maybe you can still get your room back. Everybody else's leaving."

"We gotta go back." Irmani looked up at Gib. "God's not letting me get away with it. I have to give it up for Lent."

The image of the ivory mask stayed in her mind all the way back to Jackson Square. She almost crawled back into the Presbytère. The guards watched her with trepidation, but she felt as though her strength was coming back with every step she took back toward the glass case. It was locked, as she knew it would be. The only thing that stood between her and those empty eyeholes was getting those necklaces back into the display next to the tiara where they belonged.

The curator was talking to a fat and prosperous couple that Irmani would normally have marked for a bump and grab, but all she could think of was the keys in the dapper man's pockets. She waited until he shook hands with the visitors and sent them on their way, then stepped forward.

"I found something that you want back," Irmani said. She concentrated her talent on him as hard as she could. "I'm not responsible for taking them, you understand? I brought them back. That's what counts. I brought them back. I gave them up."

The curator looked bemused but pleased at the strands of gemstones and gold that lay across his palms, though later he could never say for the life of him where they had come from or who he had been talking to. He took the keys out of his pocket and locked them away on the purple velvet next to the Comus crown and the lorgnette mask.

Irmani felt as though iron bands had been unfastened from around her chest. She stood out in the nearly empty square in the bleak February sunshine and took deep breaths of damp, cool air.

"Thank God," she said.

"What are you going to do now?" Gib asked. "We got four hours until our flight."

Irmani looked up at the cloudy sky and sighed. "We might as well go to church."

Passover

Surviving Traditions

Dr. Rachel Sternberg beckoned the rest of the xenologists into the dining hall.

"Hurry!" said the small, dark-haired woman, her eager smile framed by rosy round cheeks. "It's almost sundown. I want to start the seder service."

Dr. Carter Phillips, tall and broad with an amiable, weather-beaten face, glanced around the refectory. The big, rectangular, high-ceilinged room was the center of activity for the four-month-old exploration colony on the planet called Nong. The hall was attached to the north side of the gigantic greenhouse, a Lexan construct that was beginning to fill with burgeoning Terran plants. A couple of personal communication booths for recording messages to send home and a cabinet of board games were tucked in a corner behind the display cases full of the fruits of the settlers' discoveries, like fossil formations; preserved leaves the size of umbrellas; eggs as large as watermelons; long, fragile bones; exotic plants; and a terrarium of bright blue-green insectoids that occasionally burrowed out of the peaty mass which approximated the swampy terrain outside to peer at the humans.

Usually, the thirty or so long tables that would seat the five hundred members of the Nongian exploration crew were set in three rows of ten tables each. Now all the furniture had been moved into concentric squares, leaving just enough room for the servers to wheel trays in between. Savory aromas came from the serving hatches in the wall that led from the cramped food preparation area where the robochefs worked. Carter slung his equipment bag against the wall and inhaled with deep appreciation, trying to identify the spices floating on the air.

"Are we really going to do this?" asked Debri Sultan, with a disapproving frown on her thin face. Her narrow frame towered above Rachel's like a human exclamation point.

Rachel crossed her arms. "Yes, we are. After all, we agreed that human rights would be kept even in the reaches of space, otherwise, we're not human any longer. Passover is an important day in my religion. We have respected yours. Now I ask you to respect mine. I hope it will help you understand our traditions better. There are so few of us humans out here. We're all that we have."

"We're all scientists! These rituals have no relevance in the modern day. Why should superstitions be perpetrated beyond the orbit of Earth?"

"They're stories and traditions," Rachel said. Her eyes sparked and her cheeks flushed. Carter could tell that she controlled her temper with some difficulty. "The stories of our heritage. This is how we keep our history alive. I also want the Visitors to learn about as many facets of Earth traditions as possible, as I am sure you do. If you don't want to be here, I suggest you take your dinner back to your quarters. I don't mind if you help yourself to the *food.* I won't see you go hungry just because you won't participate in the community."

Carter placed himself between the two women before Debri could retort.

"Where do you want me to sit?" he asked, keeping his voice pleasant.

Rachel looked him up and down, but hesitated before she spoke.

"Would you mind sitting at the center table? There are only eight Jews in the crew, and we need ten to form a minyan. You've been so supportive, I'd like to designate you an honorary member of the congregation for the seder."

"I'd be happy to, Rachel. Thanks."

She beamed and touched his arm. "Bless you."

Debri sniffed and pushed past them. She went to a table at the farthest corner of the room and threw her equipment bag up against the wall next to the dishwashers. A few people followed her, all secular humanists or atheists in solidarity. They'd behaved the same way during Diwali, Chanukah, and Christmas, despite having the rest of the colony participate in HumanLight. Carter shot Rachel a rueful look and went to sit down.

"Now, if everyone will just download the Haggadah onto their tablets," Rachel said, smiling at the assembly, "we'll get started."

She wore a small, blue silk skullcap pinned to her hair, as did the other seven members of the Jewish faith. Carter found one next to his plate and put it on his head. It didn't look as though it would stay put, but it did. The other honorary Jew, Anjanette Henry, a big, busty, ebony-skinned geologist from Jamaica and devout Protestant, had pleated her skullcap and tucked it into her mass of dark hair over one ear as though it was a flower. Everyone reached for their ever-present flat-screen devices and tapped the new icon that had appeared under Documents. It opened up to display a split screen of Standard English and Hebrew. Carter scanned the English side. Syllable-by-syllable transliterations of the Hebrew prayers had been included for those like him who couldn't read the foreign text.

He and Anjanette weren't the only strangers at the inner table. Four of the Visitors, as most of the crew called them, were perched on the long benches across from the humans. It seemed odd to call them Visitors, since they were native to this world, and the humans weren't, but that was the name that the commanding officer had started calling them. Carter felt a little ashamed of himself that he didn't know any more about what was going to take place than they did.

The Visitors, eight feet tall and as skinny as ladders, with pebbled blue skin and mouths that opened vertically instead of horizontally, were always cheerful guests. With three tongues apiece, they took to new languages and musical styles like parrots. They had picked up

Standard English far faster than any human had learned their language. Most of the landing party still relied on translator devices. The Visitors didn't take that amiss. They came to regard the translators as fellow beings, and treated them with the same avuncular affection as they did the humans. They called themselves Llrrrt'dnn'iqq, a name that made sense when trilled against multiple hard and soft palates and definitely lost something in translation to the monthly reports home to Earth, hence the generic term "Visitors."

"I feel as though I am learning something about the old world here on our new world," Anjanette said, with a wry smile. "Look at this Passover plate—Pesach, Rachel called it." She touched the items in the six dished compartments on the open china platter. "All of these are symbols of the will of God. Bone of the Paschal lamb, roasted egg, greens, horseradish, charoset—that's apples, wine, and nuts—and matzoh." The last was a stack of three flat square crackers a third of a meter across that filled the middle of the plate.

Carter broke off a corner of the top matzoh and ate it. It was dry and crumbly in his mouth.

"Doesn't taste like much," he said.

Rachel reached over and smacked his hand with her fingers.

"Listen and hear why," she said, with a smile that took the sting out of the blow. "It's part of our story."

Although open fire wasn't ordinarily permitted in any of the settlement quarters, an exception was made for candles for religious or celebratory purposes, as long as a fire extinguisher was close by. Rachel stood over a three branched candelabrum furnished with three white candles the length of Carter's hand. She spread her hands above them and recited a prayer.

"Blessed are Thou, O Eternal, who has sanctified us with Your commandments, and commanded that we kindle the Yom Tov lights."

The others chimed in, "Amen." Carter hastily followed suit. Rachel lit the three candles.

"I want everyone to take a turn reading the explanations for the rituals," she said, beckoning to a cluster of youngsters who had been roped in as attendants for the feast. "First, the washing of the hands."

Two of the children, daughters of colony physician Natalie Li, brought an old-fashioned pitcher and bowl around to each of the congregants at the center ring. Carter dabbed his hands in the water and dried them on the woven towel. The white linen looked ancient, like textile displays he had seen dating back a thousand years. Embroidery in blue and red picked out the images of donkeys and flowers. He felt admiration for Rachel, who had to have packed all this gear in her shipping allowance from Earth.

Ippolita Daoud, an Israeli geologist, recited the text and prayer over eating green herbs in her guttural accent. Never good at extemporaneous reading, Carter sneaked an advance look at the file, and followed along as voice upon voice added to the explanation of the holiday of Passover. He'd never bothered with the Old Testament. His impressions, growing up in a nominally Protestant family, were that the early Jews had not really reached their pinnacle until the birth of Christ. The story of the Hebrews trapped in Egypt as a subject race proved to be painful to read, let alone voice. It gave him sympathy for the Jewish people he hadn't really felt before. He shot Rachel a grateful glance.

"Now, the Four Questions," Rachel said, smiling at the Visitors. "I've asked our new friends to participate, so they'll learn more about my religion and culture."

Mmm'ddk, the motherly leader of the most local family group, the Mmm'nnn'ilp, opened her sideways mouth.

"Mah nish-tanah ha lilah ha zeh, mi-kol ha laylot, shebachol ha lehlot …" she sang, her warm alto voice pure.

Carter looked surprised, but knew he shouldn't have been. The Llrrrt'dnn'iqq had learned Standard English without a qualm. Hebrew was just another human language. The Jewish congregation answered in the same tongue. The sung prayers were in a minor key, which in his opinion, added to the melancholy of the underlying story. He had no trouble following along, but to his ears, brought up on classical and popular music, almost all of which was in major keys, Jewish prayers sounded as alien as the Llrrrt'dnn'iqq's own trilling lingo. The only non-Jews who seemed comfortable with the prayers were of

Earth-Asian descent. Carter recalled something about their traditional music being in a pentatonic scale.

"Now, we partake of the bitter herb, Maror, which reminds us of the bitterness of slavery," Tom Rosenfield said, holding aloft a small pot of the bright fuchsia sauce like the substance on the seder plate. He spread some on a square of the matzoh from one of the baskets on the table, and ate it.

The aliens went along happily with everything. Every dish in the ritual meal had some symbolism, all of which was pointed out by various members of the small congregation. Carter tried a dab of the pink stuff. The fire on his tongue made him want to spit it out, but he swallowed instead, following it up with a drink of the unusually sweet grape wine. He had never been a fan of horseradish.

"May I have yours if you are not going to finish it?" Ddd'ohh asked. Carter always thought of the skinniest Visitor as a teenage boy. He never turned down food.

"No problem," Carter said, pushing the small dish toward the Visitor's long hand. Ddd'ohh lifted it to his middle tongue and lapped it with ululations of bliss from the upper portion of his mouth. Carter took another drink. At least a lot of wine was served during this celebration.

At last, which in Carter's estimate was at least nine hours since they had begun, but in fact was only twenty minutes, Rachel put down her screen.

"Now, we have dinner," she said, as the boxy silver roboservers emerged from the food preparation area laden with heavy rectangular pans. "Soup, gefilte fish, roast meat, carrot and prune tsimmes, kugel, salad, and, of course, more matzoh. Enjoy!"

"This is most interesting," said Mmm'ddk, making room for the soup bowl and an adapted scooplike spoon that fit into the Llrrrt'dnn'iqq's mouth. She ran a long manipulative digit down the computer file. "The Exodus, as you describe it. Human beings have such limited senses. Why did the Israelites not simply leave when they chose to?"

Rachel looked a little perturbed, her thin brows drawing down over her blunt nose. "It wasn't so easy. The land itself was hostile. Egypt is one long, lush river valley surrounded by arid deserts.

There would have been armed guards. The Israelites lived a subsistence life. They had little in the way of supplies or weapons. They were a captive population far from the land of their birth. They had small children and feeble elderly who would find the journey across the hostile sands difficult, if not impossible. When they left, it was in haste. The story of matzoh tells us that they had no time to cook, and no facility for storing food safely. The elders wanted to protect *all* of the people and get them safely out of Egypt. God held His hand over us and guided us safely out of Egypt."

"Much of this seems strange and contradictory," said Ll'ppp'rrr, the Father of Memory, or as Carter understood it, their historian. That drew a small smile from some of the group in the outer tables, until he added, "As do all of your sacred texts. Wishing for plagues does not make them exist."

Rachel shrugged. "The Torah is full of storytelling, sometimes a long while after the fact. These texts are considered to be the word of God, received through His poor, imperfect creations, humankind. This story is historical. The Israelites were made slaves by a conquering force and made to live in a foreign land. It took miracles to free them from their oppressors. Only the plagues convinced the Pharaoh that it was no longer safe to keep the Israelites prisoners and to give them permission to leave. While there was almost certainly no possible connection between the death of Pharaoh's eldest son and the Israelites, he came to consider them to be more of a problem than an asset, and let them go."

"But some of the strictures seem very strange, if God is omnipotent. The marking of the doorways—could your God not tell the difference between his Chosen People and the ones he had not chosen?"

"I suppose," Carter put in, over the embarrassed sputtering from the eight Jews, "He wanted to make sure they were obedient before he saved them. Like many things in the Bible, this might have been another test, like ordering Abraham to sacrifice his son, Isaac."

"Humans are strange," Ddd'ohh said, licking out another bowl of horseradish. He had pink streaks on his narrow blue cheeks. "But even most of your people do not see the importance of your stories."

"It is in their holy books as well as ours," Rachel said.

"So few of you agree, though." Ll'ppp'rrr aspirated the word.

"That's nothing!" Mikael Ashkenazi said, with a laugh that shook his round belly. "We're used to arguing. The saying is that if you ask eight Jews a question, you'll get twenty different answers."

"You ask good questions," Rachel said, with more aplomb than Carter would normally have given her credit for having, although in her role as a scientist, he considered her fair but fierce in defense of her research. "We're making new traditions. Maybe some of these queries should be added to the Four Questions. It will help us explain God to those who have not grown up in a deistic culture."

"Rachel, no!" Sidney Fehr protested, his dark eyes flashing under his heavy eyebrows. He was in charge of the colony archives, blog, and databases. "We don't change the traditions."

Rachel shook her head, a little sadly. "We always change, Sidney. I wouldn't be a rabbi if we hadn't changed some traditions. It's how we survive."

"Survive," Mmm'dkk said, pushing aside her now-empty soup bowl. "I wished to speak of survival! Are you prepared to survive now?" She turned to Carter and Melody Chikungwe, the settlement's co-commanders. "We have little time before you must move, or this settlement did not last."

"Will not last," Ll'ppp'rrr corrected her gently, with a trilling of the final *T*. "Your God works in ways that we do not understand. But you act with some logic. You reached out to us in friendship; let us do also. We postponed our own Exodus to the northlands to join you here. Come with us today, tonight! It is time and past time to leave this place for the season. The chh'nkh are coming. They will emerge soon from the deep swamps. Within two solar passes of their appearance, they birth their young. They will come through here soon. You must leave this place for that time. You knew of the dangers when you chose to put your homes here."

Carter felt a chill race down his spine. Placing the settlement had been a matter of discussion and argument. This was a fruitful valley, suitable as far as matters of sunlight and water were concerned. In any case, no one wanted to live in the swamps. The

Visitors warned them that it would have to be evacuated annually for a period of up to fifteen days as the predators used the valley as their hatching grounds. Then they retreated downriver with their newly borne young, not to be seen again until the next time.

The initial satellite survey of Nong had returned considerable footage of the primary predatory race. Chh'nkh reminded him of whale-sized velociraptors combined with the alien from *Alien* with its multiple jaws. Two of them had torn apart a browsing marsh reptiloid between them as though pulling a giant wishbone. The resultant gore had made a few of the scientists in the orientation hall run for the toilets.

"I thought we had more time," Rachel said.

"No more," Ll'ppp'rrr replied. "Please. It is dark now. We can escape if we hurry."

"We have taken your warning into advisement," Melody said, with a smile. "You have been generous friends. We are prepared to leave next week, as we discussed."

"The rumblings have already started," Ll'ppp'rrr said. "They are early, but must not be ignored. The chh'nkh will kill all beings that they see. If they fear for their nestlings, they will tear these habitats apart. You will not escape *later*."

It was a solemn reminder to the scientists. During the first month of the colony, two of the xeno team had hidden themselves in a blind to observe the huge predators hunting for food. An unlucky noise at the wrong moment had brought the hungry herd down on them. They hadn't survived. Carter had forced himself to view the bodies in the ruin of the shelter. It had been a horrifying mess. The only things left intact were specimen cases containing some biological artifacts and two chh'nhk eggs.

"We still have time," Carter said. "We have plenty of hydrogen-powered craft to take us up into the safe zone. If we have to, we'll load up the big shuttle, too. The chh'nkh are nowhere near us yet." He beckoned to the head of geology, who sat at the next table. "Nina, didn't you check the seismometer? We would hear the vibrations as they are tunneling upward."

"Exactly," said Nina Chessman. "The epicenter is kilometers from here."

"From within the swamps, ninety-four links from here?" Ddd'ohh asked. A link was about two meters. Nina did the math in her head.

"No, in the sedimentary formations . . ." she stopped in horror. "The spongiform peat would absorb most of the vibrations of a closer approach."

"We've been tracking the chh'nkh," Sidney said. "All sightings so far are in the delta on the other side of the ridge. There's only a narrow passage that the river goes through to the falls, and none of them have come that way. We're ready to evacuate when they start to cross."

"They won't. They travel the underground rivers to the main nesting places," Ll'ppp'rrr said, pointing to the far wall. In that direction, beyond the Lexan windows, were gentle rolling hills. Early in the settlement's first few months, Ippolita had found abandoned and unhatched eggs in gravel nests that were now on display.

"Where are those?" Rachel asked.

Nina's deep bronze cheeks paled. "Everywhere."

A roar shook the dining hall. The colonists looked at one another in horror.

"That came from right under our feet," Melody said.

"There's an underground stream directly below the building," Nina said. She pulled up a chart on her tablet and showed it to the colony chiefs. "The colony purification system draws from it for drinking water. Downstream, we drain waste into it. All the colony buildings are attached to the system. It's a big channel. The chh'nkh could swim it. It would be upstream, but they're strong."

Melody looked at the Visitors. "We thought chh'nkh only traveled overland."

"They stay below as long as possible," Mmm'dkk said, almost apologetically, although Carter knew it was their own damned fault not to have asked for more empirical detail. "Only some come by way of the pass. Their skins do not like the hot sun, but it helps the eggs to hatch."

The clattering of heavy metal brought everyone in the colony to their feet. Carter and a number of others rushed to the wide window and looked up the narrow valley. The bright orange solar-powered lights picked up movement at ground level. To his horror, the street near the hangar was *heaving*. The metal grid that served as a sewer cover shot into the air. A massive claw emerged and pawed the air. It withdrew, to be replaced by a massive, triple-jawed head with pebbled skin and wide, glassy eyes. The chh'nkh heaved and strained at the opening. The framework came away with a snap that echoed all the way along the valley. The enormous beast, twelve meters long if it was a centimeter, scrambled out of the new opening and shook itself. The metal ring hung around its neck like a torque. It shook its head. The metal contraption flew off and crashed into the wall of the laboratory building. As soon as its massive rump cleared the opening, dozens of smaller chh'nkh poured out into the valley behind it.

Chh'nkh resembled the Visitors in the same way that human beings resembled lorises. One could tell that they had descended from common ancestors, one with vertical jaws and blue skin, but had diverged long ago, with the chh'nkh evolving toward alpha predator, and the Visitors toward intelligent civilization. The chh'nkh were sheer power, killing machines made of muscle and bone. The Visitors had said that the beasts could shove aside boulders bigger than they were. It hadn't dawned on him, not really, what that meant.

They lifted their strange heads and sniffed the air. To Carter's horror, they turned and swarmed toward the hangar. The hemi-cylindrical rolled-plastic structure housed all the small travel carriers that the colony possessed, and the fifty-person shuttle they used to transit between the surface and the interstellar ship in orbit around Nong. The leader sniffed all around the big door, then let out a horrifying roar. The smaller ones charged the flimsy metal shutter. It crumpled at their onslaught like a handful of tinfoil. Carter saw the alarms that lit up on the wall screens and his own tablet. Surveillance cameras showed the chh'nhk tearing into the cabs and passenger compartments of the small craft housed in the hangar.

"They have your scent now," Ddd'ohh said.

"What do we do?" Nina clutched Carter's arm.

"Prepare to evacuate," Carter said, turning to the gathering crowd of scientists and support personnel. "On foot, if we have to.

Emergency procedures, everyone!"

The security force, twenty strong, went for the weapons locker and armed themselves with pistols and long energy rifles. Their sure movements gave Carter confidence. "Everyone, to your stations! Let's get ready to move out! Will you guide us to safety?" he asked Ll'ppp'rrr.

"It is difficult now," Ll'ppp'rrr said, opening and closing his long digits. "The chh'nkh are already here. Soon, they will sense us. Some will not survive."

"Do we have enough firepower to take all of them down?" Ippolita asked Lieutenant Ottolino, the leader of security team.

"No!" Rachel exclaimed, horrified, pushing in between them. "We're not here to destroy a native species! We're here to study them."

"Even if they kill us?" Ippolita said, scornfully. "I do not intend to die for science. Kill as many of them as we can!"

Rachel shot a look at the Visitors. "The reason we were allowed to establish an exploration lab here was because we agreed to respect the sanctity of life."

"At the cost of our own? Wipe them out!"

"That's not our brief, *professora*," Ottolino said.

"You have to save us!" several of the scientists protested.

"We are not going to wipe them out," Carter said, reasonably, patting the air with his hands. "We just need enough force to enable us to escape. Ippolita, you have duties. Rachel, you, too. Let's get to them. And so have the rest of you! Get ready to bug out!"

Rachel Sternberg put her hands on her hips. "Right. Mikael, take a loader and move as much of the dehydrated supplies as you can. See how much of the fruit in the greenhouse is ripe." The children clung together in the middle of the room. Some of them were crying. She swooped down on them. "Kiddies, help Mikael. You know he'll pick out only the boring vegetables. We want some good things, too." She clapped her hands. "Go! Hurry up! You have ten minutes."

The cluster of youngsters seemed to unfreeze. They rushed out ahead of the heavyset scientist, a few of them pulling urgently at his arms.

Kneeling beside the two little ones who were left weeping in the middle of the gray plascrete floor, Rachel gathered them into her arms. "You two have a most important job. I need you as my assistants. Come on. We're going to lock all of the doors." They struggled to their feet. Rachel took each by the hand and looked over their heads at Carter.

Do something! her eyes said.

Locking the doors wasn't going to help much, considering that the chh'nhk had just torn through the metal side of the vehicle depot, but it gave the colonists a small illusion of comfort.

"Come on, folks, we all have something to do!" Melody shouted. "Food, medical supplies, water purifiers, pest repellent, bedding, go!" The adults scattered.

Carter turned to Lll'ppp'rrr. "Do the chh'nhk hunt by scent, by sound, or by sight?" he asked. "One sense predominates in most Earth predators."

"By all, alas," the Father of Memory said, his lowermost mouth drooping open in an expression of sorrow. "They are fearsome. If you have thoughts of your God, I hope they give you comfort."

"Oh, my God, they're tearing up the library!" Sidney bellowed. "We have to get out there and save it!"

Carter ran to the window. To call the squat brown structure a library was Sidney's own description. "But that's just a massive server," he said. "None of us go in there except in clean-suits. It shouldn't smell of us."

"They tear apart everything but their own nests," Lll'ppp'rrr said, almost apologetically.

"They protect their eggs," Mmm'dkk said.

"Their eggs?" Carter blinked once. The chh'nhk overran the next building, and the next. They tore apart the barn, dragging farm equipment out into the street as though it was prey. Carter was grateful the farm animals were high up in a terraformed pasture, but how long until the chh'nhk reached them? "What about their eggs?"

"They don't destroy their own nests," Mmm'dkk said, laying her manipulative digit on Ddd'ohh's arm. "Their children are precious to them, as ours are to us."

"What can we do?" Melody asked, her usually placid face flushed. "We can't get young chh'nhk we can hold on the roofs to drive away the adults. That's inhumane, for a start."

"No, we don't need living young," Carter said, grinning for the first time. "That Pesach plate is a sign from God. Eggs! We have preserved specimens of chh'nhk eggs!" He ran to the cases. The eggs were there, two of them, the size of prize watermelons, but dark brown in color for camouflage, with the same kind of rippled pattern as the chh'nhk's skin. The stasis cubes were individually operated, so they could be opened when the xenologists wanted to examine the object.

Debri Sultan had overheard him. She abandoned the supply cart she was pulling to the rear entrance to race over to his side. She pulled his hand away from the controls.

"Leave those specimens alone!" she protested. "Finding intact eggs was almost impossible! It may be all we have left of our studies." She gulped. Her bravado didn't conceal her nerves. Carter could feel her hand trembling. "It might be all that's left for the next survey team to collect from this site."

"I want to try, Debri," Carter said, keeping his tone gentle but firm. "It could give us the chance to live until the hatching is all over. You'll find more, later. When we're all safe."

"I'm not taking that from a politician like you," Debri said, lifting her chin in defiance. "We lost people when we gained those eggs. Did you forget that?"

"And we'll lose more people if we don't try," Carter said. He stood eye to eye with the tall woman, and waited.

It didn't take that long. Debri prided herself on being logical. She turned to the stasis box and deactivated the field on one of the cells. Tenderly, she lifted out one of the eggs. Carter tried to take it, but she twisted to keep it out of his grasp. "If anyone is going to destroy this, it will be me. What should we do?"

"Like the ancient Israelites did," Carter said, with the lessons he had just heard in the seder. "We'll smear the blood from the Paschal lamb over the doorposts. Rachel!" he called to the biologist, who had her small army of children hauling blankets and bed rolls onto a skid loader. "Can you get me some fire extinguishers?"

With something to give them hope, the colonists pulled together to help.

The chh'nhk drew closer. Anjanette gave Carter and Melody a running report on what buildings and structures the huge creatures were tearing apart next. Rachel brought not only three big, red, pump-style fire extinguishers, but an enormous mixing bowl with a spout. Mikael vacuumed out the fire-prevention chemical powder. Carter took a look inside. The canisters were dry and clean.

Holding the huge egg, Debri closed her eyes for a moment. If Carter hadn't been well aware of her views, he would have thought she was praying. Then she struck the shell with the lid of one of the tanks. Albumen, clear and pale green in color, gushed into the big bowl, along with fat globules and some amorphous solids. Among them was a tiny creature, no more than two centimeters long, with bulbous eyes under translucent lids and goose-bumps that would one day have been pebbled hide: the fetus of a chh'nhk, curled around a ropy strand that must have been its umbilical cord. It had started to develop in the egg before it was put into the stasis bottle. Carter felt tears prick at his eyes.

"I'm sorry, little one," Debri whispered. Rachel squeezed her arm with a sympathetic hand.

Even though this small embryo would have developed into one of the gigantic monsters tearing apart the settlement outside, Carter couldn't help but see a helpless baby animal. This was the death of the First Born, the tenth and most terrible plague that God had visited upon the Egyptians to make them free the Israelites. Even God must have felt regret for doing it on behalf of his Chosen People, but sacrifices had to be made. Carter fished the small creature out of the bowl and handed it to Debri. Her fingers closed around it.

"We'll take it from here," he said. Together, he and Mikael beat the egg fluid into a homogenous mass and poured it into the extinguishers. "Now, all we have to do is spray it on our doorposts."

O O O

Lieutenant Ottolino stood poised by the front door of the refectory with one of the canisters strapped to his back. His fastest and most agile guard, Corporal Lisa Neuhaus, also one of the Jewish congregants, had volunteered to take the second. Carter, clad in full riot gear, wore the third. They had been monitoring the chh'nhk herd while suiting up. The next target of the predators was this building, the chem lab, or the greenhouse. Either way, everyone had to be ready to move.

Most of the adults and all of the children huddled near the rear exit with Melody and the Visitors at their head. They were ready to flee into the nearest untouched building.

"You're the co-leader," Melody argued, through the communicator embedded in the padding of Carter's heavy helmet. "You should leave this to the security personnel."

Carter shook his head, though he knew she couldn't see the gesture. "I have to. It was my idea. Just make sure everyone's safe."

Ottolino watched the video from the cameras on his wrist-mounted screen.

"Damn, they move fast," he said. Carter watched in fascinated horror as the blue-skinned giant threw up its head, listening.

"It heard you," Carter whispered. "It's coming this way!"

"Move it out!" Ottolino ordered at once. "Fire over their heads unless you're in imminent danger of death. Got that?"

"Yes, sir!" the guards chorused.

"Go, go, go!"

His second, Sergeant Randy Chen, burst out into the street, with the others in his wake. They surprised the chh'nhk by their sudden appearance, but the shock lasted only a moment. The huge leader scrambled to a halt, towering over the puny humans. It eyed the strange creatures in its path. Its triple-mouthed face nosed close. Then it opened its jaws, and sniffed hard. It let out a shriek that brought all of its smaller kin running.

Carter had never seen one up close and in the flesh like that, only partial specimens and video from drone cameras, let alone dozens. His mouth dried. He couldn't move. They were going to eat him!

"Chen! Nonlethal response!" Ottolino bellowed.

"Yes, sir!" The soldier raised the barrel of his slugthrower into the air and let off six sharp blasts. The deafening reports blasted the air and echoed down the street. The chh'nhk fled from the sound and the bright blue muzzle flashes. The whole herd, large and small alike, stampeded back toward the hangar.

The respite was long enough for Carter to regain his wits. He started spraying the door of the refectory building with thin yellow goo. The viscous egg mass was thickening up. It didn't want to come out of the nozzle, but he pumped the tank again and again to put as much air pressure behind it as he could.

"Go get the greenhouse," Ottolino shouted to Neuhaus. "Cover the whole building. They might go around the back!"

"Yes, sir!" the young woman said. She ran along the side and disappeared in the darkness.

"Dr. Phillips, you finish up here," the lieutenant said. "I'll try and cover any of the buildings that they haven't torn up yet! Get the whole perimeter. Can you do that? Sir? Can you? Are you okay?"

Carter nodded, not trusting his voice. He wondered if the Israelites had ever been as afraid as he was then.

God, if you were with Your children then, be with me now!

"Here they come again," Chen called out. He and the remaining seventeen soldiers let off bursts from their weapons, always aiming high. The blue-skinned chh'nhk ducked their heads every time the guns sounded, but they smelled food. "Keep back! Keep away!"

The predators circled around, trying to get around the source of the painful noise. Carter, too, winced at the explosions, but he concentrated on pointing the nozzle of his tank as high on the wall as he could. Yellow droplets ran down. He wiped his nose with the back of his hand, spreading goo on his face.

"Look out, they're breaking through!" Chen shouted. "Permission to direct fire, sir!"

"Negative," Ottolino said. "Unless they are a physical threat."

The next cry was a shriek. "Direct threat, sir!"

Ottolino's reply in Carter's headset was drowned out by the screams behind him. A hail of gunfire hammered his eardrums. He dashed down the far side of the huge building, pumping as he went.

At the seam where the refectory butted up against the clear plastic wall of the greenhouse, he ran almost flat into Neuhaus.

"Come on," Carter said. "Let's get the rest of the buildings on this side."

The two of them split to run around one plascrete structure after another, until he felt the pump handle refuse to move. Neuhaus came around the far corner, smearing the wall with her gloved hand.

"I ran out, sir."

"I think I have some more," Carter said. He pumped hard and waggled the hose hard. The hollow sound in the metal tank told him his was empty, too. A few drops spattered the wall. They hurried to finish the job. "Come on, let's get inside."

Carter's heart was in his throat as they cut behind the greenhouse to the rear door of the refectory. Melody opened the door to their pounding. Carter dropped his gear and ran to the front windows to look out.

He could no longer see the security team. "Ottolino, are you all right?" he shouted into his helmet mike.

"We're okay," the lieutenant said. "All but Chen … guess you could say the Pharaoh got him. I sprayed the rest of us. We're down by the residence block. You've got to see what the chh'nhks are doing! It's amazing."

The Pharaoh. That was a good description for the gigantic chh'nhk. Carter stared out of the windows. The predators reappeared, but instead of tearing up the buildings, they sniffed them carefully. The Pharaoh stalked toward the refectory. It ran its long face around the doorway, then withdrew, its eyes thoughtful. It went on to the next structure.

Instead of attacking the structures, the sauroids carefully avoided any of the structures that had been anointed with egg wash. One even chided another with a slap of its long paw when it accidentally tore into the corner of a near building that had been sprayed. They kept going, examining each building, and howling their disappointment.

Carter found himself holding his breath. Melody had her tablet in her hand. She kept scrolling up, watching one security camera after another.

"They're gone!" she cried.

The settlers hugged one another and jumped up and down, screaming. Rachel threw her arms around as many of the children as she could.

"The egg worked!" Rachel said. "A miracle."

"The Lord helps those who help themselves," Anjanette said, with a smile. "If it was a miracle, it was one that had *lots* of help."

The Visitors were delighted. "Why have we never tried that?" Mmm'dkk asked, all three of her mouths rounded with amusement. The four Visitors found themselves in the midst of a group hug.

"Obtaining the eggs is dangerous," Lll'ppp'rrr said. "But it may be worthwhile. All of us are inspired by this ritual of yours. The story of the egg and the leg of the herdbeast, and the death of the firstborn. Most interesting. It is the first of your rituals that makes sense. This will become part of our teaching chants."

"I'm honored, however you want to interpret it," Rachel said, dipping her head. She turned and eyed Debri, who stood at the rear of the crowd that had returned to the refectory. "Now, you were saying? Passover is a useless holiday? It has no relevance in the modern day?"

The biologist pushed her way forward. Carter wondered if he was going to have to step between them again.

"On a religious basis, no," Debri said, with a pugnacious lift of her chin. "On a scientific basis, perhaps … it could represent our delivery from danger. A passing over of a peril. In a purely historical sense, of course."

Rachel crowed and threw her arms around the tall woman. Debri looked uncomfortable at first, but accepted the embrace.

"Welcome to the congregation," Rachel said.

❧ Lammas Night ❧

Sunflower

Vinory dreamed again of the sunflower: tall, yellow-fringed, with a strong, thick stalk bowing slightly under the weight of its heavy head. Everything about the dream flower seemed normal, except that instead of tracking the sun throughout the day, its face followed her.

There were plenty of sunflowers in the garden outside, but why would she dream about them instead of the roses or asters or herbs? All of this place was new to her. She had come here only a few days ago. Glad for the promise of shelter against the coming winter, Vinory had not questioned too closely the circumstances under which the position of village wonder worker became vacant. Otherwise, she might have shouldered her pack and pressed on farther down the road, regardless of the holes in her boots.

Now, those boots had fresh, entire soles, and winter receded to far away in the future. Moreover, there were whole woolen blankets on the feather bed, also blessedly hers, and free of vermin, thank all gods! The three-room cottage was not merely nice, but sound, well-proportioned, and well built. It smelled of dry herbs and dust, but what of that? Half an hour's sweeping and dusting, and some of her own herbs scattered on the air or boiled for the scent had driven away the ghost of dead parsley and sage. The headman's wife had made her guesting gift of oats, tea, honey, salt, a new loaf, some dried meat, and a small crock of wine, with the promise of good food every day. Whatever she needed, they would give. Somewhere, they told her, there was a black and white cat for company, but he tended to go about his business as he chose. This could be a nice sinecure, all the benefits to stay with her, or go, as she chose, if only Vinory would at least stay through until spring. The people of Twin Streams had no one else to weave the spells to protect them from the storm or the spirits who rode it. Their last mage had died in the spring. Vinory was a gift to them from the gods, and they treated her as such.

The dream symbol of the sunflower kept preying at her mind. This was no ordinary bloom. It had a distinctively masculine presence, teasing at her with a faint, fresh-washed scent and the insouciant flaunting of mature sexuality. Did a god's presence touch the house?

If such a visitation was troubling her, she wanted to see it off! Vinory needed a whole mind and a whole heart to take care of the villagers. Some of them had been saving up a list of spells and nostrums they needed against the time that this cottage would house a mage again. Vinory would be busy from morning 'til night for weeks to come.

O O O

"Good morning, Mistress Vinory," the headman said when she came to take care of his youngest daughter, who was suffering from night terrors. Bilisa also had a head cold and was breaking out in webbing between her toes and fingers from handling an enchanted frog, but those were quietish maladies, not calculated to make her scream in the dark and wake the house.

"Now, think of something bright," Vinory told the girl, a mite of six, with big dark eyes and long braids framing a pale, moon-shaped face. "Something that gleams. Keep it in your mind." Vinory spun a disk of metal between her fingers, gathering sunlight from the beams that came in the window to store in the girl's mind. "Think of yellow, like buttercups and primroses."

And sunflowers, a quiet voice said in the back of her mind.

O O O

When the girl's mind was eased and her other problems treated, Vinory returned to her cottage and hearth. She mustn't start thinking of the cottage as hers, she warned herself, as she started a pot of porridge to cook. The mage-born really belonged nowhere in this world. They were only loosely tied to physical existence. Love of possessions made it more difficult to travel across the Veil to accomplish their spells and curses. But how easily she could get used to earthly comforts! Her cup and bowl, spoon and knife looked very homey on the mantel beside the goods of the departed Master Samon. The reflection the mirror showed her had silver threads showing near the scalp in the black wings of her hair; and fine lines ran in patterns on her weathered skin beside her dark blue eyes and the corners of her mouth. Her body would one day grow old. Would this not be a nice place to stay until the time came when she abandoned it? Hastily, she put the thought aside.

Next to the hearth was a wooden chest that Vinory hadn't dared to open as yet. It was unlocked, and the hasp was flipped upward as if its owner had been about to open it when … The villagers said that the last mage had died unexpectedly. Could it have been poison, or was the latch made of a deadly metal? Vinory prayed to be shown the truth, whispering a few words to the void.

The wind howled outside suddenly, making her gasp with its ferocity. But she saw no black spots or shining, sickly greenness on or about the lock or the chest to suggest that it would do her harm. She reached for it again.

It seemed to her that a warm hand brushed hers when she pushed the heavy lid open. *Cobwebs,* Vinory told herself. *You're imagining things.*

To her delight the chest was full of books. That made sense. It was placed handily so one could reach for a book and read by firelight. Vinory hummed with pleasure as she took the clothbound volumes out one by one and laid them on the fleece that served as a hearth mat. There was a *Geographicus Mundi*, a handsome herbal in Latin, and several books of charms and spells. Some of the books were handwritten, all in the same strong, beautiful hand, and peppered with tiny illuminations. Among the goods on the wall shelves were pots of paint and brushes made of twigs and hair. Had these drawings been the work of Samon? Then he was a scholar and an artist! She was sorry now not to have met him. And now these lovely things were hers to use. Vinory felt an unexpected sensation of warmth, as if the house gave her its blessing.

O O O

The dream of the sunflower came again that night. The seed-heavy head leaned closer to her; its leaves rustling, whispering. If the flower had had eyes, it would be looking deep into her soul. The image grew larger until it took up all of her mind's eye. Vinory woke in the dark, panting with fear. It wasn't that she disliked sunflowers, she told herself, except that the damned shells kept getting stuck between her teeth, but what was the meaning of the recurring dream? She sought peace as she concentrated on it.

Her mind had to be affected by some stimulus around her. Vinory thought again of the unseen hand that had touched her when she opened the box of books. It was almost as if someone had brushed her arm lovingly. She put her hands up into the shadows, feeling, sensing. The air was empty, as it was supposed to be.

Movement near the fire startled her. Vinory sat upright to see what had thrown that shadow against the wall. No one else was in the room with her. It must be the cat, she told herself.

No. The thought came unbidden. Vinory started.

There *was* a consciousness here. Who—or what—was it? Vinory crawled from her bed and flung a cloak around her, determined to learn more. From her basket, she took a thin copper ring and a thread, and crouched by the fire. She set the pendulum spinning, catching glints from the faint embers.

"Are you malevolent? Do you mean me harm?" she asked the pendulum. Without hesitation, the ring began to rock back and forth. No. Twice. And the shadow fluttered into the light again.

"Who are you?"

That question the pendulum could not answer. The intruder could have been from anywhere and any time in the beyond. Vinory reached outward with all the delicate fingers of consciousness that she used to touch the other side of the Veil. The presence seemed to have a connectedness to the place in which it was now. Was it an entity called here by the previous owner of the cottage, or an unfortunate spirit tied here by who knew what bonds? She couldn't guess what had gone before. Perhaps in the daylight she could peruse the books and notebooks for a clue.

An unexpected rush of air flowed past her cheek and brushed her hair. Chilled, Vinory crept back to bed and tucked the blankets around her.

O O O

She treated the presence with careful reverence, in case it was the tendril of a god's mind. When Vinory rose in the morning, she greeted it, and put the first crumbs and drops of her breakfast on a dish to one side as an offering. If it was not a god, then it had another name, and she meant to find it out. As she worked on a charm for a spinning wheel for Lenda, the village fine-weaver, they chatted idly.

"What sort of man was Samon?" Vinory asked, tying threads together through the spokes of the wheel.

"Oh, he was a fine-looking man," Lenda said, rocking her plump self back on her three-legged stool. "Not as big as some, but with white skin like a girl's, and dark eyes and lashes that looked painted on. I wanted to picture him as a tapestry, but he wouldn't let me make an image of him. Said it tied him down."

"That's true," Vinory said. "How did Samon die?"

"Caught a chill sitting up for six nights in a row to cure a sick child," Lenda said. "Or at least, that's what I thought it must be. The next day, I was bringing him food, and found him. I thought he was sleeping, but he was dead. Not a mark on him. Such a shock it was." Lenda clicked her tongue.

"Six nights! Such devotion to healercraft," Vinory said, impressed. "He must have been most caring."

"Oh, well, any man would do the same, since it was *his* child," Lenda said, peering at the mage-woman under her heavy lids. "The girl he got it on was too young to marry, our headman said, but plenty old enough for dalliance among the daisies at the spring planting, in Samon's eye. Said it was the god's doing. He shouldn't have taken her, but what could the parents say? You can't make a cow back into a heifer."

"Oh," Vinory said, disappointed. "Too true." The wretch. Her image of a lost scholar and saint tarnished around the edges. Technically Samon had been correct. Mere mortals could not dictate whom the god said should play the spring queen in the planting dance, but one could temper his whim by leaving unwed children out of the range of choice. Had the god stayed around too long after the dance, and swept Samon away while leaving a thought-shadow in his place?

"No, indeed," Lenda said, reminiscing. She sounded fond of him, as she stared past Vinory through the door at the bright autumn sunshine. "Couldn't keep his hands to himself, no, not if they were tied behind him. He needed a strong woman to keep him in line. Not that women here aren't of sound mind," she added, warningly, in case Vinory would think they were all vow-loose, "but none *wanted* to say no to him."

I could, Vinory thought.

The presence teased at her the next day as she rooted through the cottage's storerooms. It seemed to have a courtier's manners, going here and there with her, moving aside while she was walking, crouching close as she knelt to examine a box or basket. It certainly was not a god, since when Vinory had chosen to ward herself the night before, she was not troubled by the dreams or the mysterious touch. Instead, Vinory could feel the presence hammering unhappily at the wards she had set up, pleading to come in until she drew a veil across her thoughts so she could sleep. Who or what could the presence be?

"I don't know whether it would have been a pleasure to know you or not, Master Samon!" Vinory said, sorting through a bag of dyed threads. "Dallying with children, though I grant you lived up to your responsibilities afterward. You stood right on the fulcrum of the Great Balance, didn't you?" The presence said nothing, but she was beginning to feel that it might indeed be Samon lingering there.

What *had* taken his life? Over the years, she had sat up many nights with patients. Sometimes she'd caught what disease they had, but she always manifested the usual symptoms. The women said there were no signs at all, and yet Samon's soul had fled. Vinory's mind spun with unanswerable questions. Could Samon have been ripped from his body by some powerful force? A curse? Could what happened to him happen to Vinory? Should she flee this place while she could? No wonder the townsfolk were so desperately glad to have her stay.

When she went to bed that night, she surrounded herself with wards and protections so thick that the cat couldn't find a place on the bed. He hunkered down next to it, grumbling.

The next morning, the sun poked a gleaming finger through the curtains of the cottage window and tickled Vinory's nose until she woke up with a sneeze.

Goodness, she thought. *I hope I'm not coming down with Bilisa's cold.* A few experimental sniffs proved that her nose was clear. That was a relief.

The cottage was tidied nearly to the homey stage. Vinory though that today she would ask the fuller or the blacksmith for a little polishing sand to shine up the fine metalwork that decorated the doors and cupboard fastenings. That would be the finishing touch that would make all perfect. She could perform some small service for the craftsmen in exchange, but so far everyone had been too shy to ask their due. The courtesy would pass soon enough, Vinory knew, so she would keep offering so as not to seem arrogant in her power.

Vinory thought a slice of meat and some broth boiled from the dried meat would taste nice this morning. The black and white cat wound between her feet while she put the pot onto the fire and made her toilet for the day. She gave him a piece of the meat. He gulped it down and begged for more.

"There, now," she said, picking up a cloth to swing the hook holding the pot out of the fire, and flicked it at him. "You've had your bounty. Go and catch something for yourself. Fresh meat's better for you anyhow." The cat sat down and nonchalantly washed his shoulder to prove to her that he didn't care. Smiling, Vinory ladled broth into her bowl and took it and the remains of the loaf to the table.

Beside her plate was a yellow flower. Vinory hadn't noticed it before, but that did not mean it hadn't been there when she arose. She was touched by the gesture, thinking that a villager had decided to show her a kindness by leaving her a posy of autumn flowers. Then she took a close look at the bloom. It was a daffodil. Another sunflower, not heavy with autumn, but fresh with the dew of springtime. She'd always known it as a gage of the laughing young god, in his youngest and most playful incarnation. And yet, she reminded herself that the dancer was also faithless, flitting from woman to woman, whoever would have him. There were no daffodils in the village. They withered by May. July was long past their season. Who had reached through time for this lovely thing?

I, the voice said. *I would please you.* The warm touch brushed her hand again and encircled her wrist with a lover's touch.

Vinory started, afraid. Samon *was* still here, and not only was he tied to this place, he was now tied to her as well! Abandoning bowl, loaf, and hunger, Vinory rushed out into the sunshine.

At least the ghost didn't follow her beyond the walls. She ran down the hill toward the fields where all the able-bodied villagers were helping to bring in the hay. The good folk greeted her gladly, offering her bread, cheese, and meat from their own breakfasts. She accepted only enough to keep her from getting lightheaded.

"Now you're here, will you bless the coming harvest, lady?" the blacksmith said, leaning heavily on his scythe. He swept a hand around to show her a valley filled with dusty gold and dark green. Poppies of that astonishing red clustered at the edge of the cropline.

"How hard you have worked," Vinory said, sincerely. The villagers straightened up with pride. "Of course I will give the blessing. The gods have been good to this place. It will be a bountiful year. I need a handful of each of the young produce." Two boys ran off and came back with handfuls of grain, fruit, and tiny, perfect vegetables. Vinory exclaimed over their beauty. "Good. And now I … I need wine, salt, a small bowl, and a crust."

There were a few odd glances exchanged, and one or two people looked up the hill at her cottage, only a few hundred yards away.

Vinory was ashamed to admit she was afraid to go back for her basket, so she waited and smiled politely until somebody gathered the components of the harvest prayer for her. At least her knife was in her belt.

Beckoning the workers together, Vinory sprinkled salt in a circle around them, then advanced to the sunrise side with the wine and bread. The headman, who had witnessed many a harvest rite, came forward with a large, flat stone, which he set down at her feet. Chanting the ritual words, Vinory poured the wine into the bowl and crumbled the bread into it. She held the bowl to the sky, and let the Veil open ever so slightly.

The powers of nature were formidable, but most folk saw only the merest wisp of that influence. It was only during rituals and festivals that they had the opportunity to see what Vinory and the mage-kind saw every day. The headman and his villagers were agog as a mouth opened in the sky and drew the wine and bread up to it in a garnet stream. A beam of light issued down on Vinory and her makeshift altar. The offering was acceptable. Now she filled the bowl with the fruits of the harvest. As she continued her chat of praise and entreaty, the golden light covered the bowl. In a blinding flash, the offering was gone. The light faded into Vinory, leaving her glowing in front of the stone, ponderous with the weight of godhead. She was silent for a long time. The villagers waited respectfully until she spoke.

"The gods hear us, and they are pleased," she said, feeling both god and goddess resounding in her chest and brain. "Blessed be this place and these people. The work that they do shall prosper."

The villagers muttered, "thanksgiving," and Vinory ended the ritual by touching the point of her knife down to the flat stone, earthing the gods' power as a symbol of the unity of the planes. When she broke the circle, she drew a little of the godhead into herself to protect her as she walked back up the hill to the cottage. It was hers now. She had earned it. No ghost would dare to keep her from it.

The bread on the table was stale now, and her broth was gone from the bowl. The cat must have lapped it up as soon as it cooled. Vinory's movements were abrupt as she prepared another meal to restore her after the drain of rending the Veil.

The spirit presence was immediately at her elbow, offering concern. She pushed away at it with her thoughts, trying to find some peace to think. The spirit kept trying to get her attention.

"Leave off!" she said, irritably. "You're worse than the cat." It drew back perceptibly, hovering near the book chest. Vinory ate her meal and took a little rest on the bed with her back propped up against the wool-stuffed pillow. The presence stayed at a distance from her, but she could still feel its regard.

"What do you want?" she demanded at last. Protected by the fragment of light, she let her consciousness open up to the presence. Immediately a sensation of need flowed over her. Vinory raised the godhead as a shield, and the presence withdrew a little. It continued to broadcast to her its feelings: pain, fear, frustration, and despair.

"You are trapped here," she said. "That I had already guessed. But what do you want of me?"

Her soul was suddenly flying, feeling wings stretching out to either side of her, feeling the air cupped beneath them as strong as a hill. Terrified, Vinory threw up her shield and cowered behind it. The sensation stopped at once. The spirit sent contrition, and she glared in its direction.

"You wish to be free," she said.

Beside her on the bed, another daffodil appeared, fresh and golden yellow. Vinory reached for it, but her fingers stopped halfway. She could sense the spirit's anticipation, but she was afraid.

There were spells to free spirits of the dead who had become trapped in a place. But she did not dare to try one of them without knowing how it was Samon met his end. Could his fate drag her along with it? Neither the headman nor her neighbors had mentioned anything haunting this cottage before her arrival. She, the mageborn, must have reawakened him. Now he radiated hope towards her.

"Go away," she said, leaving the flower untouched on the blanket. "I must think."

Ignoring the desperation she felt at the perimeter of her consciousness, she drew up wards of protection that she wore all day.

O O O

"Oh, yes," the blacksmith said, scooping polishing sand into a cloth for her. "Master Samon demanded the best from us, but he gave champion service. Saved my cow when she was in calf with twins. Told me his price was I owed him ironwork for a year after that. I saved no money. He had gauged exactly how long it would take me to pay off two more bullocks. Ah, well," he said, twisting the corners of the cloth into a knot, "fair measure's fair, after all."

"What about the child he left?" Vinory asked, tucking the parcel into her basket. The blacksmith put his own interpretation upon her question.

"She's all right. Shows no sign of acting like one of the mage—like one of your good folk, lady. Just eight months old, she is. The girl was much too young when he picked her to dance the spring goddess with him, just into womanhood, but she's turned out a good mother for all that. She's wed to my son, now."

O O O

Fair and foul, Vinory thought, as she lay abed that night. The spirit offered caresses and favors, but she kept him firmly at arm's length. *Every one of the folk here have a story to tell about him. He's trustworthy. He's not. He's generous. He's mean. I don't know what to believe. And none knew how he died.*

O O O

"He was kind, mistress," the girl said. The house was small but very tidy. In a corner, a baby slept. Vinory glanced at it and noted the dark eyelashes and hair, unlike its mother, who had hair red as a fox's fur. "He was good to me, so kind and gentle-like. The husband he got for me isn't nearly as … nice to be with. Though he tries." She gave a helpless shrug, and a shy smile.

The girl lifted her sleeping infant for Vinory to bless. Halfway through the incantation the child woke, and watched her with eyes far too wise for its age. They reminded her of the sunflower.

O O O

Over the following days, the spirit of Samon kept up its wooing. Every time she sat down, it was at her elbow. It stood at the end of her bed at night, and attended her at table like a servitor. She began to find its constant company oppressive.

"I can never be alone with my thoughts while you're here," she complained to the invisible presence. It had grown stronger and more distinct as the moon waxed. Tonight the moon was nearly full. She could almost imagine she could hear Samon speak from the other side of the Veil. She shooed him away so she could think.

Vinory had now been in Twin Streams two weeks. In another two it would be Lammas. She began to think of the harvest festival. It would be nice to have a strong male to play the corn king in the reaping dance. Vinory had studied all the available men, and confessed herself disappointed. The only really attractive man of exactly the right age, Robi the tanner, had a jealous wife whom it would be bad to cross. The blacksmith looked likely, too, though he was very heavy-handed. Vinory was speculating idly on the identity of her partner, because it didn't matter whom she liked. The goddess would choose for herself when she possessed Vinory's body. Luckily there was no such stigma on a young man as there was on a young woman joining the sacred dance. If he could perform, he was old enough.

"I could dance the autumn and the spring with you, if you set me free," the spirit told her that night in her dreams. Vinory felt the warm touch of a man's body against hers, strong muscle, questing hands. She squirmed against the caresses, enjoying them. She brushed against a smooth swell of muscle, which shouted, "Yow!" Vinory's eyes fluttered open to see the cat scooting across the floor between her and the fire, tail lashing furiously.

I'm just dreaming about the dance because I was thinking about it today, she told herself. *Because I'm lonely.*

When Vinory settled back to sleep, she forgot again to raise her wards. A tall, dark-haired, dark-eyed man came to her and showed her visions of the times he'd led the dance. He was graceful and slim-legged, with broad shoulders and narrow, strong hands that he used to lead his partner to and fro in the complicated patterns. Vinory felt herself tapping her feet, wishing she could join in. It looked so tempting. The man paused within arm's reach of her. She called him by name.

"Samon?"

He turned as if to answer, stretching out a hand to her, his eyes agleam … Then she woke up, with the fitful light from a lantern in her eyes.

"Sorry to wake you, mistress," said Tarili, the baker. "My wife's baby's coming. She needs you. The baby's turned wrong."

"I'll come at once," she said, groaning. Vinory roused herself, and let the dream fade from her mind as she gathered her medicines and paraphernalia. She could now feel the presence standing in the corner, disappointed.

O O O

When she returned after daybreak, exhausted, the spirit resumed its campaign to get her attention, hovering around her like a bee on a lilac bush.

"Oh, go away, Master Samon!" she groaned, half asleep already. "I'm too tired to argue with you."

"That's why I'm pushing you now," he said, to her dreaming mind. "Wouldn't you like to have someone to warm you? Winter is coming. You could have a babe of your own next summer."

"I have a dozen babies! The villagers' children are my responsibility. You must not tie me down." She could see his face again, an inverted triangle of ivory, with those dark, long-lashed eyes. She was afraid even in her dreams, but tempted. Samon was very strong-willed. And handsome.

When she woke several hours later, she was refreshed, and also resolute. Samon was dead. She, Vinory, must stay alive and clear her mind. That meant banishing the spirit who continued to trouble her.

She felt panic. But knew it at once it wasn't her own.

"If you won't, or can't, go on your own, then I must help you along," Vinory said, brutally. "It's only logical, Master Samon."

The presence sought to get between her and the book chest, but she just walked through him, ignoring the psychic shock she got from the contact.

She had seen a spell for setting free a trapped spirit in one of the handsomely made volumes that Samon had scribed for himself. Vinory thumbed through the books until she came to the one she remembered. It was a harsh enchantment. The rebound of the working would be hard on her, Vinory knew, but she would be rid of this nettlesome presence who awoke all sorts of feelings in her that she had no time for. She had what components were needed at hand. The text said the working must be done on Lammas Night. After that, he would be free, and so would she. She felt lucky that she had not come after Lammas. Otherwise, it would be a whole year before she could send him away.

The spirit's panic was stronger than ever. Then, as she watched, the very pages of the tome turned over one by one, past the banishment spell, to another text. Vinory bent her head to read.

It was almost the same as the first, ridding a place of a troublesome spirit—but by locking it again into human form. The difference between the two spells was only a single word. She looked up involuntarily, as if Samon was sitting there across from her.

"You want me to re-embody you?" she asked. Feelings of joy and hope washed over her, then retreated at once, lest she chide him again for overwhelming her consciousness.

I could do it, Vinory thought, rereading the text. *But do I want to? Samon has had his life—he's led it! But was his work done? Do I dare to make that decision, for or against? I serve Nature. But do I want so strong a man to push me out of my place just before the weather begins to turn?*

Perhaps, she was not as young as once she was; the thought of sleeping in cold caves and under the brush at waysides now bothered her. *You're getting soft,* she told herself. *You're becoming too earthbound.*

I was not earthbound enough, the presence felt at her. *I lost my hold. It was too soon. Help me! It is my will.*

She read the spells again, both of them, hoping for clues to what she should do. The spells lacked reference to the high gods, and took part of her as well as of the one who sought reinstatement in life. Were these evil spells? Would she imperil her soul by performing one or the other? And yet, she had to do something, or the dead mage would drive her insane with his fretting and pleading. Either banish or restore, but she must do one of them, no matter what it cost her. To harvest one must sacrifice, so the Lammas rite went. But did she want this harvest? A mage who was neither good nor evil, and yet neither dead nor alive. And yet, he was a living being, deserving of her aid.

O O O

Vinory's sleep was troubled by Samon's entreaties. "I will hold you in honor," his spirit said in her dreams. He dropped to his knees before her, the dark eyes pleading. "I will give you pride of place, and let you lead in all things, if I may live. Oh, lady, let me through!"

Honor. Samon could see all her thoughts. He knew the turmoil in her mind. How could Vinory hide anything from him? But did he mean it?

"I … I don't know if I can trust you, Master Samon," she said at last, conscious even though her body was asleep. "I'm afraid of what admitting you back into life will mean to me. I dare not undo what the gods have done. You should go on to the Summerlands beyond the Veil."

"Not yet! Oh, I will be kind, lady. On pain of eternal condemnation, I swear it. I will give you all honor."

"How can I believe it?" Vinory asked. "You'll say anything so that I will open the Door on Lammas Night and let you through instead of banishing you forever."

"See for yourself," he said, taking bother hands between his as he continued to kneel before her. The impishness touched his eyes, and she felt like melting. He was so very handsome. "If I lie, you can take other revenge upon me. To be mortal again has its own discomforts. It will at least be as interesting to stand with you, for fair or foul."

She took chances; why else would she be a witch and a mage if she was not ready to face the unseen and call the unknown by its name? A challenge like that appealed to her more than any of the blandishments, but she was still uncertain.

"I will think about it," she promised.

O O O

The candles burned as she swung open the cottage door to allow the night breeze to enter. The villagers of Twin Streams had gone off to enjoy the rest of their harvest night. Now she was left with only one task to do. The spirit of Samon waited at the perimeter of the room, full of fear and anticipation as to his coming fate, for it was tonight or never.

All the materials Vinory needed were laid out. She lit each one of the candles in turn, praying to the gods that what she was about to do was right. The warm breeze caressed her bare skin as she chalked the circle on the floor and stood inside it. She took up the book and read aloud from it by the light of the candle in her hand. Her voice trembled through the first syllables, then grew stronger, though she felt the pull of unseen forces at the very stuff of her existence.

The golden light broke from the candles at the points of the compass and joined together to form a ring of fire which grew and grew until she was surrounded by it. And then it died away, leaving an arch at the north side of the circle. Through it she could see a shadow. It was a mature man with dark hair and eyes, and milk-pale skin. He smiled at her tentatively. She knew at once that this was Samon. She must send him away or answer his plea *now*. There was no more time to decide.

"I will give you all my honor, no matter what you decide," Samon said. He looked hopeful like a puppy who did not dare to wag its tail. "May I come, or must I go?"

He held out a daffodil to her, as a token of the beginning of new things for both of them. *At least, it would be an interesting life from now on,* she thought. A considerate lover, so the girl had said. He would have to be, to make up for the part of her life the restoration of his life would take. Vinory smiled. For fair or foul.

"Come," she said, and held out her hand to him.

HALLOWEEN

Trick

Creak's bright-yellow eyes slewed desperately around the twilit lawn. His shroud was gone. He should never have turned his back on it for a second, but that brackish puddle full of icy cold water and decaying autumn leaves had been just too tempting. Without hesitation, he'd slipped off the shining white cloak and slid into its depths. Once he'd finished reveling in its delightful chill sliminess, he had discovered the shroud was missing.

What could he do? Without it he was a pair of disembodied eyeballs in a blob of invisible ectoplasm floating about three feet off the ground, unable to groan, shriek, fly, or cause mischief. Not properly terrifying for Halloween. Which this was.

Creak rolled his eyes about again, scanning trees, bushes, houses, and cars, in case his shroud had only fluttered to the ground. Wait, there it was! On the other side of the hard path mortals called a "street." The wind must have picked it up. He glided across, passing through automobiles, giving minor hallucinations to the humans within, and swooped gladly on his cloak. But it was not his! The one he had doffed was moonlight spun into fine silk by silver spiders and woven by witches adding spells to the weft as they went. *This* was coarse, wrinkled *cloth*, only called white out of courtesy. And the eye holes! Crudely hacked into the cloth, two gaping wounds, not the round wells of loss, fear, and despair through which Creak gazed at the world. Some being, he was now sure, had seen his beautiful shroud and stolen it, dropping this in its place.

Creak felt outraged. He must find the thief and punish him!

But where to begin? Now that Creak concentrated, he perceived that both sides of the street were filled with mortals. As was proper for the sacred day, the short ones were clad in outfits to mimic the beings who crossed freely between the worlds of the seen and unseen: goblins, witches, vampires, even a blue and red outfit meant to represent a spider … but mortals had an odd perception of reality, after all. And many ghosts. Creak flitted after the first one. Its cloak was not his, but rather like the one he had found on the ground. Grumbling, he scooted back to the discarded shroud, looking for clues.

A child dressed as a pink fairy spotted his glowing eyes and screamed. Creak was gratified. Even without his mystic cloak he could still inspire awe and fear. Her father, clad in a warm jacket and the ubiquitous leg coverings mortals called "blue jeans," shot over to see what had frightened his offspring. Creak stood his ground, but suddenly noticed a religious emblem about the man's neck. In the possession of a true believer, amulets had the power to banish his kind to the unseen world for a hundred years. Without his shroud Creak was vulnerable. Quickly he snatched up the crude cotton robe and put it on. The man saw him embodied and stopped short.

"Oh, honey," he said to the girl, "it's just another kid dressed as a ghost. Come on."

He hauled her away by the hand, but she kept looking back over her shoulder at Creak. She knew what she'd seen.

Now, to find the thief.

O O O

"You shouldn'a taken that other kid's ghost costume," eight-year-old Brianna Cole scolded her one-year-older brother Jay. Her Little Mermaid costume slid down her shoulders inside her fleece coat, and she stopped to put her plastic pumpkin of treats on the ground to hike it up. "Jay!"

The formless white shape halted impatiently on the sidewalk. The sides of the sheet bulged out as though the boy underneath it had put his hands on his hips. "What?"

"It was mean. Besides, it's stealing."

"I didn't steal nothing," Jay said, his voice sounding sepulchral and far away. "I traded."

"But you didn't ask first. That makes it stealing. What do you think Mom's going to say when you come home with that costume instead of yours?"

"Hah!" Jay snorted. "She'll never notice the difference." Brianna considered. That was true. Mom never did notice stuff, which is why Jay always got away with things. "It's way cooler than mine. The eyes are round and the cloth's so light it's like it's not really there. Come on, let's haunt Mrs. Springer."

Brianna hoisted her pumpkin and hurried up the front steps of the old frame house after him. Mrs. Springer always gave full-size candy bars. The Cole children never missed visiting her.

Jay reached up and pushed the button. Deep inside, they heard the clang of the bell.

The door swung open. Mrs. Springer, a nice older lady with pale gray-blond hair who always wore tweed skirts, peered out at them. In one arm she held a big crockery bowl. "Well, well, two scary visitors! What can I do for you?"

"Trick or treat," Brianna chorused obediently. But Jay decided to ham it up. He raised his arms and wailed.

"Whoaa-aaaa-oooo!"

Mrs. Springer let out a strangled scream. Her eyes went as round as her glasses, and she retreated into the house, slamming the door.

"What did you do?" Brianna demanded. "She had Snickers!"

"Me?" Jay asked, hurt. "I didn't do anything. Hey!" he shouted, raising a cloth-covered fist to pound on the door. "Trick or treat! We want our candy!"

But to both children's surprise, his hand passed straight through the polished wooden panel. Brianna gasped.

"Hey, cool!" Jay said. He withdrew his hand and tried it again. He thrust his foot through. "Wow. This costume must be magic." His happy voice scared Brianna more than his newfound ability to pass through walls.

"Jay, we're gonna get in trouble!"

"No, we're not," he said, turning his blank eye holes toward her. "Look. I'll go get our candy, and we'll go to the next house."

He turned his back on her protests, and walked straight at the door.

His eyes knew the wood was solid, but he slid through it with no more resistance than if he was walking through water. The shock was the change in temperature. It was bright and warm in Mrs. Springer's hallway. Everything in it was decorated in cheery red checks, and it matched, unlike the decoration in their house.

On a gingham-covered table by the door was the huge bowl. It was filled with candy bars: Snickers, Mounds, Crunch, Laffy Taffy, Chuckles, and York Mints. Jay chose a Crunch bar and put it in the pumpkin bag under his costume. He heard Mrs. Springer's panicky voice in another room. He eyed the bowl, and decided to bring it outside so Brianna could take her choice. That courtesy ought to sweeten her disposition and make her stop nagging him about taking the other costume. It was only a trick, right? This was Halloween. Trick or treat.

His leg went through the door all right, but the bowl in his arms would not pass. The shock of it striking the door surprised Jay. The bowl tilted off his hands and fell backward *through* his body, crashing to the tiled floor and dumping treats all over.

"Oh, *hurry*!" Mrs. Springer's voice cried. "I think it got into the house. It's horrible!"

Jay didn't hesitate. He dove through the door.

"Where's my candy?" Brianna asked, as he rushed past and down to the sidewalk.

"She's calling the cops," Jay said. "Come on, we've got to get away." Alarmed, Brianna fell in behind him.

"What did you do?"

"I broke the bowl. It was an accident!"

"You better go back and tell," Brianna insisted. "And pay for it."

"Tomorrow," Jay panted. "I swear. I don't want to get thrown in jail. Let's just keep trick or treating."

Brianna groaned, but it was no use pushing him. He'd keep his word to own up; he always did.

The next house was past a big hedge. Jay stopped being nervous the moment they were behind it. Mrs. Springer couldn't see them any more.

"Hey, guess what?" Jay asked, as Brianna concentrated on lifting her skirts to climb the stoop. "I can fly in this thing! Look at me!"

Brianna refused to turn around. She rang the bell. "Trick or treat," the children chorused together.

Mrs. Park, a Korean woman who did crossing guard duty, slowly put down her bowl of treats and opened the door, holding out her hand to Brianna.

"Come in here, honey. This is a Neighborhood Watch house. You be safe until you mama come fo' you."

"Why?"

"There a bad thing behind you." She screamed something in Korean over Brianna's shoulder. "Now hurry come in call you mama." She grabbed for Brianna's wrist.

"Run, Brianna, she's a pervert!" Jay cried. Brianna scooted out of reach of the little woman's hand, and stumbled down the stairs after her brother. Mrs. Park squawked out another diatribe behind them.

O O O

Creak floated up and down street after street. The mortal who had taken his shroud could not know all of its powers, therefore it could not have gone far. Its principal talent was the spreading of fear and awe, so he must look for the center of the greatest disturbance in this area. With the borrowed robe dragging along the ground, he wove as quickly as he could in between the groups of mortals on the sidewalks, sensing ahead of him for strife and turmoil.

O O O

"What did we do?" Jay asked, desperately, as they cut through the backyard hedges to the next street. The man who had answered the next door didn't say a thing, but reached for a shotgun—a shotgun!—from next to his armchair, and sprang up to chase them. "Is he still following us?"

Brianna looked back. "I don't see him, but I hear noises. Everyone's coming."

"We've seen a monster!" voices behind them shouted. "It went that way! Hurry, help us! Call the police!" Footsteps crackled through the brush as they emerged on the far sidewalk.

"I've gotta get rid of this thing," Jay panted. "Something about it's *wrong*."

"It's stolen magic, that's what," Brianna said.

O O O

The disturbance was heaviest here. Coming around the block from the opposite direction, Creak spotted his beloved shroud at once. A boy running toward him was wearing it! Creak could see the uncouth movement of breath puffing out the hood. The mortal was afraid. Good. Perhaps he was ready to return the stolen shroud now.

Creak shed the heavy, crude cloak on a bush in plain sight.

O O O

A crowd of adults burst through after the two children. "Look, another ghost suit!" Brianna yelled, pointing.

Jay threw off the borrowed costume. It was whisked away before it hit the ground, and he caught a mysterious glimpse of yellow light. Not caring what became of it, he dove for the sheet on the bush. "It's my old one!" He managed to shrug into it just before a policeman sprinted ahead of the group of pursuing adults. He grabbed Jay by the shoulder and turned him around to show Mrs. Springer and the others.

"Is this your specter?" he asked. "It's just a little boy, folks."

"Well, I thought it was a monster," Mrs. Springer declared, as the officer pulled the costume off. "Oh, it's Jay Cole. I'm sorry, honey. I don't know what I was thinking. Probably been watching too many horror movies."

Jay put on his best pathetic face, the one that kept him out of trouble at home. "I'm sorry I broke your bowl, Mrs. Springer!"

"How'd you get through the door?" she asked. "It was locked."

"Uh, it was a trick. You know, trick or treat?"

The older woman put her arm around him. "It's all right, honey. I never liked the darned thing. Come on back to my house and I'll give you both a bunch of candy bars."

"Crunch is my favorite," Jay said. Brianna followed him, rolling her eyes.

O O O

Creak followed them, too, floating along easily and invisibly at their heels in his silken robe. The boy needed a lesson in respect. He'd wait until Jay was tucked up in bed, maybe wait until just before midnight, and then he'd teach him what haunting was all about.

Smiling Jack

Rebecca Jenner jumped off the hay wagon onto the uneven ruts of earth behind her boyfriend Don Giatelli. The dry, gray soil caught at her Nikes, making her stumble. A gust of chill October wind lifted her light brown curls. She wished she'd worn a hat.

"Look at the size of that pumpkin!" Don exclaimed, ignoring the knee-high gourds all around his big, sneaker-clad feet. He headed straight for an orange-red fruit as big as a La-Z Boy recliner ridged with furrows as deep as Rebecca's hand was long.

"Don't touch it, kid," Mr. Barrow warned him. The weathered-faced farmer sat on the tractor seat and leaned an elbow on the controls. "You gotta look out for the ones who're rocked back on their haunches like that. The mouth at the bottom's smilin' at ya. It'll getcha. That's why they cut 'em into Jack o' lanterns, takes all the power outta 'em. You wait until tomorrow, when I cut it open to get the seeds out. Then you can touch it all you want."

The pumpkin did seem to be smiling at them, the blossom end that would normally be resting on the soil puckered into a mean grin. Rebecca recoiled, but Don patted it anyway. Barrow gave him a sour look. Clearly, he thought he was wasting his time driving all the way out with just two teenagers. "All right, choose the ones you want, and let's go."

"He's cranky," Don whispered, as they climbed back into the hay wagon with their chosen pumpkins. "Let's come back tonight and make him sorry he was mean."

O O O

A full moon shone over the big open field as Rebecca climbed out of Don's crowded car. Four of their friends had listened to Don's plan to get even with the bad-tempered farmer, and decided they had to get in on it.

"Come on!" Don whispered, as Rebecca hesitated. The others ran out ahead of them and started kicking in the unharvested pumpkins.

"It's creepy," she said.

"It's just a pumpkin patch. Hurry. Raree and the others are already having fun!"

"Don, this is vandalism," Rebecca protested. "We're destroying private property."

He gave her a withering look. "It's an old tradition, and it's just fun," he said. He ran off to join the others.

Pieces of shell and wads of pulp, ghostly gray in the moonlight, flew all over the field. Rebecca followed reluctantly, her arms folded over the little purse on the long strap across her body. Raree Tondal, the high school's prized 7'2" basketball forward, drew back one incredibly big foot, and kicked a huge pumpkin halfway down a row. It bounced and split into three big pieces. The others cheered. Raree held his hands up in a victory clasp over his head.

"Shhh!" Luis Olmedos hissed. "The old guy'll hear us!"

"So what?" asked Mark Greenberg, laughing. But the boys lowered their voices. The only sounds were calls from the occasional night bird, the rush of car tires on the tree-lined roads surrounding the field, and the *thud-gunch*! of a shoe penetrating the shell of yet another pumpkin.

"Hey, pretend they're the asses of the cheerleaders," suggested Carlos Cruz, pointing a finger at a row of basketball-sized gourds. He was notoriously unlucky in his attempts to get any of the girls to date him. "That one's Cheree," he said as he booted the first one. "This one's Marylou …"

Rebecca turned away in disgust. She could have told him why none of them would ever go out with him, and it started with deodorant. Angrily, she stalked over the deep furrows toward Don, who was going down a row of small white pumpkins, decimating them like Godzilla walking through Tokyo.

"Grrrh!" he growled, waving his arms. "Grrr-ooough!"

"You're really enjoying this, aren't you?" Rebecca asked.

"Dude, what's your problem?" he asked her. "Go kick something! It's fun!"

"I want to go home," she said.

"Soon," Don said. His legs were covered up to the thighs in gleaming pulp. "C'mon, you try it." He pointed at a small globe on the ground between them. "C'mon, just a little one."

"No. I don't want that junk on my shoes."

"God, you're dreary," Don groaned. He booted the little pumpkin. It rolled down the row and split, lying with its seeds leaking out like entrails. "Wow, look at that one!" He moved toward a huge sphere tilted sideways, its surface a zebra pattern of dark and light.

"It's freezing out here," Rebecca said, disgusted. "I'm going to sit in the car."

He ignored her, marching down on his prey with purpose. Rebecca glanced around. Carlos had hoisted a huge gourd over his head. He staggered a few paces, and heaved like a shot-putter. But a vine caught his leg, ruining his timing. He dropped the pumpkin almost on his feet.

"Dammit," he swore, jumping back to avoid the splatter of goo. Undaunted, he went straight for another, bigger fruit.

Boys, Rebecca thought in dismay. Why wasn't she at home with her girlfriends, painting jack o' lanterns on their toe nails for tomorrow night's Halloween party? She had a great costume, Trinity from *The Matrix*, all black vinyl and cool shades. If she caught a cold standing out here in a field in the middle of the night and had to miss the party, Don was a dead man.

The moon made eerie shadows across the fields as it ducked behind a veil of cloud. In the diminished light Rebecca couldn't see either Raree or Mark. Carlos and Don had joined forces to ruin two rows of head-sized pumpkins leading up to a file of humped giants.

The keys were in the old Delta 88, just where Don had left them. Rebecca cranked the ignition, relieved to see the blue light of the speedometer. The big engine sounded deafening after the silence of the field. Suddenly scared at the loneliness of it all, she turned the radio up full blast. Rage Against the Machine howled out of the car's four speakers, and Rebecca leaned back with her head against the seat rest to enjoy the music.

Pretty soon, the radio station turned over to some dreary ballad. Rebecca twisted the ancient silver knob off. How long had they been in the field, anyhow? The longer they stayed, the more likely it was someone was going to come and maybe arrest them for trespassing. She'd better go get the guys.

A dire chill wind whistled up the arms of her thin coat as she got out of the car. She peered over the field, but could see no movement in the faint silver light.

"Don?"

No answer but the whisper of leaves moved by the breeze.

She pursed her lips in annoyance. They'd seen her get out of the car, and they were pulling a joke on her.

"Come on, guys, this isn't funny! Tomorrow's a school day, remember? Let's go!"

Morons. They knew perfectly well she had to wait for Don or Luis to drive the car. She didn't have her license yet. So she had to play hide and seek with them. Ugh. Boys.

I will not scream, she thought, as she tiptoed along the rows full of twisted vines. *I will not scream. They're going to jump out at me and yell "boo" But I will not scream.* The trouble was, the more she insisted to herself that she wasn't going to scream, the more she knew if one of them did jump out, she was going to shriek her lungs out, just like those stupid girls in the horror movies. All right, so it was kind of fun, waiting to see who was going to pop out first.

"Luis? I know you're there. C'mon, Raree…"

Something caught her eye on the ground. It was Luis's striped scarf, almost draped around a big fat, drunken-looking pumpkin the size of an ottoman.

Carlos had asthma. She ought to be able to hear his breathing. She closed her eyes and let herself drift, going toward any noise at all, picking her feet up carefully so as not to trip on the obstructions she bumped into. The night was so silent she could hardly stand it. When she got home she was going to put her Walkman headset on full blast and drive out the memory.

Something cold and smooth touched her outstretched hand. She jumped backwards before her eyes flew open. She squinted in the faint light. It wasn't a boy hunched over like that; it was one of the pumpkins. The giant, the one that Mr. Barrow had told them to keep away from. She had no intention of getting close to it.

But in the moonlight the half-seen smile compelled her. Her feet lifted one at a time, drawing her nearer and nearer to the huge, ridged fruit. The grin called her forward. She wanted to run away, to scream, but her whole attention was focused upon the pursed mouth that now opened and spread wider and wider. A musty, damp smell issued forth from the heart of the gourd. How could it do that? It must be a trick of the light. She would just go back to the car now, where the boys were waiting. It was a joke …

The cold lips suddenly touched her flesh. Rebecca gasped as the pumpkin sucked her inside it like dust in front of a vacuum.

O O O

She lay curled up on her side on a damp surface clutching her head protectively between her arms. Her body felt as though it had been dragged through a life preserver, bruised on every side. She hadn't seen what she had just seen. It had *not* happened. She was *not* inside a pumpkin.

Rebecca rose to her knees. The scanty moonlight would have seemed like carbon arc spotlights now. It was so dark that she almost doubted her own existence. Gingerly, she put out a hand in the dark, and withdrew it right away as cold wet strands draped themselves around her fingers.

"Brrrr!" she exclaimed. But she forced herself to try again. Summoning all the courage she had, she made her hand go out through the sticky spaghetti, until it touched a wall that stretched all the way around her in a huge sphere lined with wet fibers and almond-shaped stones.

"This can't be happening," she said aloud. Her voice resounded, trapped as it was inside a solid object. "I've been eaten by a pumpkin!"

She sat down as the horror of that truth overwhelmed her. It had eaten her! And now, was it going to digest her? Would the farmer find bones inside when he came to cut the seeds out Halloween morning?

He knew that this could happen! He had said so. Rebecca battered at her memory to recall everything Mr. Barrow had told them when they had been there earlier.

The mouth on the bottom of the tilted ones could get you; that she remembered. That's just what had happened. She had gotten too close. She was doomed!

Frantically, she started pounding and punching the hard sides. "Don! Luis! Help! Someone come and get me out!"

She carried on until her hands were sore and trembling. She kicked at the shell. It must be too thick for her soft shoes to dent. But where were the boys?

Realization hit her as hard as her own situation: they had set out to destroy every unpicked pumpkin in the field, without paying attention to what position they lay in. They must have gotten too close to smiling pumpkins and been trapped, too.

She didn't dare wait until morning for rescue. The digestion process could start at any moment. She didn't want to die. Tears filled her eyes, but she dashed them away with an impatient hand.

What else had Mr. Barrow said? They cut pumpkins into Jack o' lanterns, to take away their power! If she could cut through the shell, it would have to set her free!

Her nails were already hopelessly broken. She reached into the pockets of her jacket and jeans. Her old Girl Scout knife was sitting uselessly in her bureau drawer at home. If she had the power of Phoenix, of the X-Men, she could summon it here, or just use Nightcrawler to *bamf* her out of there. But she wasn't home. In the dark, she turned her purse out into her lap. A paper-covered tube—that was no use. A stick of gum; her mouth was dry, but if she chewed that gum, she'd heave, she just knew it. A hard, rough finger-long piece of metal as cold as the side of the pumpkin—her nail file!

Where to start? Was any part of the shell thinner than the others?

It didn't matter. She felt her way to the nearest upright wall and stabbed at the center with the file.

The big pumpkin seemed to move around her in agony. Rebecca shrieked as wet strands and seeds dropped onto her neck. She shoved them away and kept cutting. The side she was slicing at began to shed water as though it was bleeding. For a moment she was grateful for the darkness. She didn't want to see it bleed all over her. Wet, the file slipped in her hand, gouging her as she grabbed to steady it.

"You're not going to get me," she snarled at the pumpkin. Tears ran down her face. She took off her jacket and wound it around the blunt end of the file, using it as a handle. Resolutely, she cut and cut and cut. The point hit something stiff, like cardboard. Rebecca pushed. Suddenly there was no resistance. She had gone through!

Rebecca lengthened the slit. When it felt about a foot long, she changed direction, cutting at a 120° angle to the first cut. And when she had finished that, she joined the ends of the two with a third. She rolled onto her back. With her feet, she shoved at the triangle portion. It moved, then shot away from her with a horrible squelching sound. A wave of cold air came rushing in. She clambered up and crawled for the opening. Fibers grabbed for her as she scrambled out into the moonlit field. Rebecca controlled her fear until she was on the cold, rough dirt. She crawled away on hands and knees, goo and seeds and strands of pumpkin guts clinging to her all over. She took a moment to breathe, then she stood up. The others were trapped inside pumpkins, too. She knew that. She had to save them.

Only the smiling ones were carnivorous, so the farmer had told them. Rebecca ran back toward the fruit she had seen wearing Luis's scarf. It wasn't very big; could a whole teenage boy be inside? She sawed away at the shell with her file until she heard a cry from within. As soon as she shoved the point through the shell, the pumpkin split, and Luis was lying on the ground in between its two halves.

"My god, Becky," he gasped, staring up at her. "What happened?"

Rebecca dragged him to his feet and explained as quickly as she had while making for the double row where she had last seen Don. "Only the smiling ones, got it?"

"Got it," Luis said, fervently.

They located only two smilers in the row of giants, sitting side by side. Under the shadow of one was a sneaker a lot like the ones that Carlos had been wearing. With Luis helping, they broke open the pumpkins. Don and Carlos rolled out, panting in fear.

"Oh, baby," Don said. "I thought I'd die in there."

"I think I had an accident," Carlos said, looking down at his pants. Rebecca groaned.

It took a little longer to locate where Mark and Raree had been marauding, but only moments for the four of them to break out the other two teens.

"How'd you figure it out?" Don asked, giving his girlfriend a grateful hug. The two of them were slimy with pumpkin guts.

"It was what the farmer said," she explained. "About Jack o' lanterns. The tradition of cutting faces in them must have gotten started to protect people from being eaten."

"Too smart," said Raree, with an admiring grin.

"That's why she gets straight A's," Don said proudly, putting his jacket around her. Her hands were shaking so much she let him fasten the coat up for her. "I should have listened to you in the first place. We're going to have one hell of a story to tell the others on-line tonight, and it's true! Come on. It's late. I'll drive you home." He guided her toward the side of the field. The moon had come out again, lighting up the windshield of the old Delta 88.

"No," Rebecca said, firmly, stopping in her tracks. "Before we go, I'll help you destroy the other smiling ones." When Don raised an eyebrow, she shook her head. "Maybe that's how the tradition of kicking in pumpkins got started, too. Self-defense. We don't have time to carve them all."

❧ THANKSGIVING ☙

The Stars in Their Courses

hundred turkeys," said Captain Daniel Holcomb.

"No," said Quartermaster Betty Jackson.

"Fifty."

"No."

"Twenty?" Holcomb asked, becoming more exasperated by the moment. He leaned over the white enamel table to glare at her. "Dammit, woman, this is for the crew's mental well-being."

"I'm thinking of their future well-being," said Jackson, imperturbably, sitting with her arms crossed. "These are our brood flocks you're so blithely decimating."

Dan Holcomb, captain of the Earth colony ship *Columba*, didn't consider himself unreasonable, but he disliked being at a tactical disadvantage. A rangy, sandy-haired man whose height was all in his legs, he was sitting when he should have been standing, the better to get the others' attention, but sitting was more of an authoritative posture, and that was important just now. He regretted deeply making this a public meeting, but too much had happened in the last thirty-seven days to make it a confidential discussion. All important discussions needed to be held out in the open, or rumor would distort all the good that came out of them. There had been too many rumors lately shooting around on the internal s-mail system, and too much back room politicking in chat rooms, break rooms, and bedrooms. The mission to Gamma Taurus was in danger of coming apart from internal pressure.

The other department heads sat around the table, flanked by anywhere from three to eight supporters, but Jackson, opposite him, was his only serious rival for loyalty from the ranks. She was an attractive, petite brunette with amazingly beautiful flower-blue eyes fringed with long, black lashes. Holcomb had a problem keeping his own eyes off her. During cryosleep his berth had been right next to hers. He wondered what kind of dreams he might have had about her in that slowed-down state. Thank God that no one had yet worked out a way to read people's thoughts. She was not only an excellent officer, but a warm, compassionate person. People confided in her. One of her young lieutenants, after an impromptu counseling session with her, had nicknamed her the Mother Superior. The title had stuck, which bothered Holcomb. He'd been raised a Roman Catholic, and had trouble reconciling the nun name with the attractive thirty-year-old female to which it was attached. Her expression at that moment would have suited a nun, prim, disapproving, and unyielding except to her own higher authority.

The fact was that by official charter she held autonomy over her department. Only by calling it an emergency could Holcomb overrule her, and a ritual pig-out was not an emergency. But everyone was looking forward to the celebration so much that he was trying hard to get her approval on releasing the appropriate stores. It wasn't easy.

"How many have we got in cold sleep?" he pressed her.

"Five hundred. But," Jackson held up a warning hand to forestall his protest, "that's nothing. A small family could eat one a week. We have four hundred and seventy couples on board. We need two, maybe three generations before we have sufficient genetic redundancy to blow the minimum count for one day."

"I know the statistics, Jackson, as well as you," Holcomb said, with some asperity. "Five, then. One percent of the total."

"No. No way."

"Then how many will you allow for the feast?" Holcomb pressed.

"None!" She ran a long-fingered hand through her hair. It was very nice hair, and Holcomb enjoyed watching the way it fell into stylish untidiness. "I can't. Really."

"You approved of this plan from the beginning," Holcomb pointed out. Jackson threw up her hands.

"All right! So, I agreed that this Thanksgiving feast would be a good thing. But we can't allow our present exuberance to threaten our future survival by using up seed vegetables and breeding animals for one dinner. For pity's sake, we haven't *landed* yet."

Holcomb knew he was risking valuable resources on what seemed like a wasteful notion, but the crew was getting restive and fragmenting into mutual complaining societies.

He blamed it all on Mission Control back on Earth. They'd ordered everyone into cryosleep too soon after takeoff, before Holcomb could unite everyone under his authority. And now the travelers had been wakened too soon, so they had too much time to think about the upcoming landing, and to begin to jockey for position, trying to establish beachheads of personal power before they touched down.

Such struggles, in the myriad turnings of the quarter-mile-long ship, undercut Holcomb in small but significant ways. He felt every day as though he was losing more ground. That could not continue. Small political groups had formed all over the ship, competing for advantages, and obstructing members of other groups from obtaining needed information or supplies. Those who tried to remain uncommitted to the groups quickly found that no one trusted or cooperated with them. Politics could be the death of the colony effort. To give Jackson credit, she had always kept her department operating as it was supposed to, though Holcomb sensed a personal snub. He disapproved. He needed all his officers behind him, not forming little fiefs to usurp his position.

But the problem was what to do about ship's morale. The fragmentation was threatening the colony effort. So much so that Holcomb was being forced to make hard decisions. Earth had entrusted command to him. He was not only captain of the ship, but would be the first governor of the Gamma Taurus Four colony. He would hold the office for five years, after which the colony would be allowed to replace or re-elect him as it chose, but it appeared that he might not get the chance to govern. There was an undercurrent of distrust and discontentment. Holcomb had no ideas of his own that could undo the damage and restore the cooperative spirit that had imbued the settlers before they'd gone into cryosleep. He had asked his officers for suggestions.

It was dour-faced Rodney Campbell, head of Engineering, who had come up with the eventual solution. He had approached the captain to insist that the symbolism of the approaching event of landfall could not be ignored. It ought to be observed with a ceremony of prayer and thanksgiving for having made the journey safely all the way from Earth.

Holcomb was intrigued. Here was an opportunity to reunite the crew behind a common cause, a fact that had gotten lost in the grab for power. They were the first Earth ship to set out into the void, beyond the bounds of the Sol system, to make a new life for humankind among the stars. They should gather together and celebrate that miracle. A thanksgiving was the answer the captain had been hoping for. Holcomb immediately set the idea before his officers. They were less interested in a ritual, but brightened at the notion of a food-oriented celebration, and gave him a rousing round of approval. Now all they needed to do was figure out how to make it happen.

So they were here, around a long table in the middle of the rec hall, the largest single chamber on the ship, each with their copy of Campbell's proposal printed out on translucent plastic flimsies. Holcomb looked out over a sea of gray-blue cloth. Word had spread about the captain's plan. Every crew member who could jam into the room was there. The rest of the sixteen hundred settlers and crew were watching on screens all over the ship. Holcomb had to make a strong showing here.

"We can't serve everyone shipslop for Thanksgiving dinner," Holcomb said. His own supporters nodded their enthusiastic approval. One of the other reasons that it was a shame they had been awakened so soon was that it extended the period they would have to subsist on ship food. Those purees and biscuits were not exactly hardtack and swill, but in an earlier century forcing the crew to eat them for six months on end could have provoked mutiny. They contained every nutrient the human body needed: fiber, protein, carbohydrates, fats, vitamins and mineral supplements, but the flavorings always seemed to be somewhat off. In fact, thinking of Thanksgiving, the turkey paste was far too salty and tasted faintly of paprika. Holcomb would order that no paprika be involved in any way during the cooking process. "Everybody misses real food, and I should say few lose out on a chance to say so."

"And I can't allow valuable brood hens to be slaughtered," Jackson said, firmly. "Request denied. Find alternatives. In fact, you are going to have to find supplements or alternatives for most of the foods on this list." She shook the plastic flimsy at him.

Murmuring broke out around Holcomb. How dare she flout his authority there in front of the entire crew? He felt his face go red, lighting up his freckles like neon spots. Jackson looked abashed, and ducked her head.

"I'm sorry," she said, looking up into his eyes again. "My mouth got the better of me. I apologize, Captain." Holcomb nodded. He could still pull success out of this discussion.

"One," he said. "One turkey. That way everyone can have a taste of the real thing. It's the symbolism."

"Yes, yes," insisted Campbell, his head turning toward her as slowly and inexorably as that of a tree sloth. He addressed her in the ponderous way that he used to lecture the ensigns on how to replace modules. "It's the event that's important! We are about to set foot onto the soil of a new world, as much as many of our ancestors did onto the continent of the Americas. I believe that we need to commemorate that in a vital and sacred way, to impress upon us the importance of what we have undertaken." Jackson smiled.

"That's a lot for one poor little turkey to accomplish." She eyed Holcomb. "On a ten kilo bird, allowing about half for waste, you're talking about a five-gram sample per person. Is it worth it?"

Holcomb could feel the avid anticipation of every man, woman and child on the ship behind him as he said, "Yes."

O O O

"I've got a problem," the Mother Superior said, appearing at Holcomb's office door with an armload of plastic sheets. Holcomb jumped up from his desk and gestured to his personal easy chair. He'd always intended that when he became governor the big, black leather recliner would be his official seat.

"Please sit down, Jackson," he offered. She grimaced.

"I'm too agitated to sit. This food thing is going too far. Everyone is giving me wish lists for the kinds of food they want to see on the table. If I approve all the requests for samples of sweet potatoes, cranberries, pumpkin pie, green beans and onions, corn and biscuits, we are not going to have any specimens to plant when we get to Gamma!"

"I've got the entire Biochem department working on artificial constructs," Holcomb said. "They need real examples to test against. You'd be impressed by the process."

"I know," said Jackson. She sighed. "I've been down there eight times this week. They've requisitioned half a ton of soy kibble and powder, chemical extracts and esters, and I wanted to make sure what it was going for. I have to ask you to insist that they not waste anything they're taking."

"I'm sure they're not," Holcomb said, frowning. "Lieutenant, they have to experiment on something. I told you that if we spared the real thing, we were going to have to offer something almost as good in exchange. Otherwise, what is the point?"

"The point is that this whole exercise is either too early or too late. Three days until this feast, and then what? Another forty days until landfall. Will it hold them? No meal is *that* filling. I mean, figuratively." Jackson plumped down into the easy chair, and bounced her bottom on the cushy padding. "Say, this is nice. What does it weigh?"

Holcomb felt himself blushing again. "Half my personal luggage complement," he admitted.

"Suited to your lofty position?" she asked, and gave him a self-deprecating grin. "Sorry, that was a low hit, Captain. I seem to be always socking you in vulnerable places these last few days."

"More than you know," Holcomb said softly. She caught his gaze with an expression of surprise, followed by a look that

Holcomb could only feel was a summing-up. He hoped he passed her standards. Both of them were aware that the contract they had signed required them to marry and raise children with *someone* once the colony was settled. Holcomb wanted Jackson to be his mate. He had been aware of his feelings toward her a long time, but had almost always suppressed the thoughts because the business of running the ship got in the way. Similar thoughts must have run through her mind, because her lips parted slightly, but she turned hastily and hurried out of the room without speaking.

He watched her leave with great regret. If only they hadn't been in rival positions. If only the office of governor had been a permanently appointed position that he could give up when he felt the colony had reached a secure point. Five years was too brief a time to establish a safe, viable colony from scratch. On the other hand, he could understand Earth government being reluctant to trust anyone giving up the office willingly. It might even be hard for him, but right now he had to hold fast to his job. Too much depended upon him.

O O O

The *Columba* was due to break out of tesseract within three days. The upcoming event caused Executive Officer Donaghue to change the bridge technicians' shifts to 13 hours out of every 24, instead of the usual 8 1/2 hour shifts. There were no complaints over the schedule. Everyone was enthusiastic about it. Those present would see for the first time, on spectrascope, of course, the invisible halo of solar radiation around Gamma Taurus that marked the edge of the heliopause.

Holcomb, who had risen through the ranks as a navigator, spent days overseeing the data pouring in from the sensors, and checking out every system to make sure they would take no harm as they passed inside the barrier. No one wanted to leave the tesser bubble intact going through. For one thing, it was believed to be dangerous. For another, everyone wanted to see the system already.

At the speed they were moving they'd pass through the Oort cloud in five more long-shifts, and reach the fourth planet, their new home, in forty days. Telescopic views would be possible soon. Everyone wanted to be the first to spot Gamma Four, so Holcomb had to order crew members off the bridge when their shifts were over, or they'd fall asleep in corners with their eyes open.

Late at the end of the extended first shift on the third day, the navigational computer said they were where they were supposed to be. Holcomb gave the order to drop out of tesseract. The nearly silent-running engines that had steered the ship for the last eighteen light years raised their voices to a whining pitch that slowly died away, replaced by the heavy thrum of impulse engines. For the first time since just outside the Sol system, stars appeared in the tri-dee screens. The largest, Gamma Taurus, was a ruddy-yellow disk floating in space dead ahead. The nav program drew the elliptical orbits of her attendant planets and asteroid fields around her.

"There she is, people!" Holcomb exclaimed, pointing at a bright quarter-crescent no larger than the head of a pin. "Land ho!"

The crew cheered wildly. Holcomb stared at the curved dot. That was their new home. As he watched, he imagined he could see it growing larger. They'd be there soon. For a moment he understood what Campbell had been trying to hammer into his head with his lectures about Plymouth Rock, Thanksgiving and the Puritan pilgrims. A new world, full of promise, and it was all theirs. For better or for worse, they were on its doorstep. He took a deep breath, and let it out slowly. The bridge had fallen silent.

He looked around. Every tech on the bridge was doing the same thing he was: staring at Gamma Four. They gave him sheepish grins. He waved a hand at them.

"All right, you've seen it. Exec, set up a slide show for everyone on the s-mail system. Don't let it be said that we hogged the view all to ourselves. Even though we were the first." He gave them a conspiratorial smile. "All of you not on shift, go to bed!" He glanced at the chronometer on the wall over the viewscreen and headed for the hallway. "That includes me. Good night! We're almost there!"

They gave him another cheer that was abruptly cut off by the sliding metal door. Holcomb headed for the lift down to his quarters. After the hubbub on the bridge he enjoyed the quiet hum of the empty corridor. The peace lasted for five seconds before someone grabbed his arm and turned him in the opposite direction, steering him toward the next set of lifts. He looked down to see the petite woman, her eyebrows drawn down toward her nose.

"Jackson! What's wrong?"

"I'm smelling it again," she said. "I told you before, and they're at it again."

The door opened on level five, and Holcomb had to admit she was right. Straight out of the lift, he could smell it. Sautéed mushrooms with garlic. He closed his eyes and inhaled a blissful lungful of the aroma.

"Illicit stir-frying," Jackson said, furiously, dragging him toward the Biochemistry lab, past a sad-faced ring of protesters carrying signs saying, "Spare the Bird," and "No America-centric Imperialism in Space." "I *told* you they were misusing my samples."

"They're *eating* them, Jackson," he said, trailing behind her, a large freighter towed by a small, angry tugboat. "What's wrong with that. You didn't want them to waste anything. What do you expect them to do with the leftovers? Compost perfectly good food?"

"They insisted they needed a second five-kilo box. And now I know why!" With Holcomb in her wake, she slapped in a senior-officer code override on the lock and burst into the laboratory. Guiltily, the twenty or so crew members wearing white coats over their blue shipsuits jumped back from the wall-mounted heating chamber, four or five of Holcomb's officers among them. Sure enough, inside the heater there was a glass retort full of ivory-brown slices and white dots partly submerged in bubbling liquid. Jackson grabbed it out, too angry to feel the heat of the container that turned her palm red.

"So you *have* been stringing me along. I believed you were working on a breakthrough. It was just a ploy to get into the supplies!"

"But we did it, ma'am. I mean, we didn't. Here's our product, ma'am," a young tech said, offering her a container of gray paste. She struck it away with the side of her hand, too mad to taste it. The captain gestured him over. The young man turned to him with a grateful look, offering a stirring rod as a spoon. Holcomb took a taste. The earthy taste spread over his tongue.

"It's good," Holcomb said, intrigued. He fished one of the pieces of hot mushroom out of the beaker Jackson was brandishing, and compared them, becoming more delighted with each taste. "By heaven, it's exactly like real mushrooms. Good job, Perkins, is it?"

The stocky tech beamed.

"Yes, sir. Thanks."

Holcomb pointed with his makeshift spoon. "How's this stuff with garlic?"

"Not so good yet, sir," Perkins said, "but that can wait for a while. We just wanted to make sure the compound would hold up in the oven. For the stuffing."

"So you *are* finished with the mushrooms?" Jackson asked. The techs nodded. "Then why didn't you return the unused vegetables?" she demanded, shaking the beaker at Perkins. "I could have harvested the spores from these and put them back in storage!"

"Well, ma'am, we didn't think of that, exactly. I mean, you released them. We didn't think we would have to give them back. We thought it'd be okay." The young man was shamefaced but defiant. "Come on, ma'am, it's been months since we had real food, and all this stuff was just sitting there. With respect, ma'am, you're obsessing."

"That's it!" Jackson said, rounding on Holcomb. "You hear that? They don't appreciate conservation of resources. I want you to assign the techs in charge of manufacturing foodstuffs for the Thanksgiving dinner to me. I want temporary authority. I need to run this personally."

"These are *my* people," Science Officer Thompson exclaimed. The redhaired woman pushed forward out of the crowd. "Captain!"

"But they're working on *supply*," Jackson said, "and that is *my* department. If they work directly under me I will see to it that waste is prevented."

The door slid open.

"Save the bird! Save the bird!" Suddenly, Holcomb and the others were surrounded by the crowd of protesters who had been outside, brandishing their signs. Some of them picked up beakers and headed for the disposer unit. Perkins and some of the other techs sprang forward to stop them, and got involved in a scuffle to retrieve their experiments.

"Aw, dammit, who let them in?" Thompson complained, yanking retorts out of the hands of a yelling woman.

"What's going on here?" Holcomb boomed, ducking out of the way of a sign that swung dangerously close to his head.

"They're vegetarians," said Campbell of Engineering, standing up from a stool in the corner. "They are protesting the death of the turkey for the Thanksgiving roast. I have tried to explain to them the necessity for the sacrifice, but they do not listen to me. That's why we locked them out."

"Captain, you can't turn over my people to another department," Thompson protested. "I'll need them!"

"Quartermaster Jackson's authority would extend only to functions relating to the project, Thompson," Holcomb said. "She does know her stuff. It won't stop her using anyone who wants to help. Will it, Jackson?" he shouted over the yelling protesters.

"What?" she shrieked from the corner where she was holding the beaker of mushrooms over her head. The science technicians pushed the protesters out the door and shut it on them. Perkins entered a locking code, and turned his back on the banging at the door.

"You'll let anyone help who wants to, right?" Holcomb shouted, into the newly restored silence.

"Not everyone," Jackson said, putting on her Mother Superior expression. "There won't be room in here or in the galley for anyone but the techs making the food and the cooks preparing it."

Immediately, there was an outcry from the people left in the room.

"Look, Captain," said Lieutenant Dermott Colwabe of Hydroponics, a dark-skinned man with one of the few beards on the ship, "everyone wants to cook. We all want to help out. This is supposed to be a celebration for all of us."

"Well, everyone *can't* cook," Holcomb said, reasonably. "We're all going to eat. Won't that be enough?"

"No!" "What about my ideas?" "My mother's peach cobbler …" "Green bean casserole …!"

The captain gestured for silence. He knew he was favoring Jackson unfairly over the other officers. "I'm sorry! There's only so much that needs to be done."

The protesting officers surrounded him and Jackson, all shouting at once. The argument went on and on, growing more acrimonious and personal. Jackson's face grew red, and Holcomb saw another outburst brewing.

"Quiet!" Holcomb shouted. "Quiet! All right, that's enough! What no one here realizes is that our very survival depends upon our remaining as one group! This is not beanball, people! We are entering into a potentially hostile environment, away from all support from home. We have only ourselves to rely upon, and we need to be able to rely upon one another. Now, we have one further choice that no one has suggested. I have enough ni-gas left over to put us all back into stasis. I can turn the ship around and take us home again. I would rather do that then land sixteen hundred people I know won't survive on an empty world."

"You can't do that!" one of the technicians exclaimed, her mouth hanging open. "We're less than two months from planetfall!"

"Oh, yes I can," Holcomb said, in a stiff voice. "If this is the way you cooperate, it would be better than landing. A decision like that'd be the end of my career, but I'd sooner have that happen than watch every one of you die because you won't accept the responsibility that goes with the risk!"

"With respect, Captain, you haven't been showing the kind of leadership we need," Thompson said, nervously. "We've just been filling in."

"All right, I accept that," Holcomb said, swallowing his indignation. His own Science Officer was speaking out against him. In a way he was glad they would never go back to Earth. He'd hate to have the brass hear that. "That was a mistake. I admit it. But the mark of true leadership is the ability to delegate."

He aimed a thumb over his shoulder. It was an offhand gesture, and he hoped Jackson wouldn't read it as an insult, but he didn't want to meet her eyes just then. That would be too distracting, and he needed to be the only authority on this vessel at this time. "Jackson is in charge of cooking. If you want to work in that department, speak to her. Colwabe"—the Hydroponics chief looked up—"you're in charge of setup and decoration. You've got plenty of material. You can use dead leaves and stuff. Look in the library computers for images. Anyone who has unfulfilled creative urges can work with you. For once we're not going to eat in shifts, and that means finding extra room. Fit as many tables as you can in the rec room and the mess hall. All others will have to be seated at tables in the connecting corridor. Knock yourselves out, so long as the décor is recyclable. If making paper chains is beneath them, send them to Galman. She's in charge of cleanup." The assistant medical officer nodded curtly.

Holcomb turned to the chief engineer. "Campbell, I have a special job for you. I am putting you in charge of serving. Get your people into the proper mood, and they can explain the meaning of every single dish if you want them to. I suggest you enlist the ones who have cultural or philosophical disagreements with the menu or the holiday. Nothing makes for a good dinner party like a little controversy. Your choice." All of them looked disgruntled, except Campbell, who looked grimly pleased with his assignment. Holcomb raised his voice over the murmuring.

"I expect you all to fulfill these functions, along with your other jobs, which I expect you to do perfectly. You're right. It is only 40 days to until we make planetfall. We want to be ready to get off this boat as soon as possible, and that means having everything done on schedule. We want to have a great party, yes, but dinner for sixteen hundred does not negate the importance of the landing we're supposed to be celebrating, or has everyone forgotten that?"

Holcomb had to stifle a grin. The shamefaced expressions on some of the faces around him told him they'd done just that. The crowd melted away, leaving only the hard core, the department heads and the chief rabble-rousers. "I'm giving these assignments to you, and I leave them in your hands. Any questions, come to me. Keep me posted on progress. That is all." He fixed the stragglers with an unblinking gaze, and suddenly, they remembered other appointments, too. He raised his eyebrows at Jackson, and left her alone with Thompson and the other techs.

O O O

Holcomb was just climbing into a clean uniform when the communications beeper on the wall of his quarters started sounding.

"Holcomb," he said, with a sigh, slapping closed the fasteners on his chest. He wasn't even on shift yet, and here was the first crisis of the day.

It was Thompson, her eyes intent. "Captain, you have to get down here!" He heard shouting in the background.

Holcomb groaned, but he kicked into his ship boots, and headed for the Biochem lab.

"What are those?" he demanded, pointing at a cluster of large, shiny, brownish objects on the table.

Jackson and Campbell looked up briefly from the argument they were having. Thompson left a counter full of beautiful pseudo-pumpkin pies and hurried to the captain's side.

"They're the turkeys, sir," the Science Officer said. Holcomb surveyed them. They didn't look like turkeys, and he'd helped his mother put together Thanksgiving dinners and Christmas lunches since he could stir stuffing. He wagged a finger at one, fishing the word out of his memory.

"That's a cornucopia," Holcomb said, "and those two are shaped like pumpkins. What is going on here?"

"Ensign Riga, sir," Thompson said, gesturing toward a stocky blond male with callused hands. "He's a woodworker. He had this idea for a shortcut, a really novel approach to shaping the soy turkeys with a laser saw. And, since we've got about fifty of them to make, we let him try. It starts with a twelve-kilo, block of pressed meat substitute, half light and half dark, and it does a pretty good job. Well, about three hundred hours, the computer glitched. It was reading a three-dee image of a turkey, but it skipped over and started carving roasts in the shape of the next piece of clipart in the file. And then the next. So, when we came in about oh-seven, this is what we found."

"And why is Jackson blowing a gasket?" Holcomb murmured, watching the quartermaster snarling at the chief engineer.

"It's Commander Campbell, sir," Thompson said, lowering her voice. "He thinks the cornucopia is a more appropriate symbol of the event than a turkey. After all, it's the symbol of abundance, and we aren't going to find any turkeys on Gamma Four that we don't bring there ourselves. He wants *all* of them like that."

"Well, there's plenty of room in them for the stuffing," Holcomb said, "but you're right. Everyone else is going to be expecting the ordinary turkey shape."

"That's what I said!" Jackson exclaimed, turning toward him. "You see?"

"Well, I can't help it!" Campbell said. "We can't reshape them now!"

Holcomb stepped between Jackson and Campbell.

"They ought to look like turkeys!" Jackson insisted, glaring up at him.

"These are perfectly fine for serving," Campbell insisted.

Wincing, Holcomb held up his hands. He turned to Jackson. "I know." He turned to Campbell. "No. We're doing it the way it's been done on Earth for four hundred years. Problem solved?" He smiled at both of them. "Good. Because I need to get up to the bridge."

Campbell scowled at him. "Your favoritism doesn't become you, captain."

"It's not just favoritism, Commander. I was just thinking that one day I hope to have a lot to be grateful for, and one way I mean to get there is by working for the good of the many over the good of the few. You're outnumbered, and I am just casting the deciding vote. Is your staff ready for its part of the feast?"

"Not yet," Campbell said, sulkily.

"Then, I strongly suggest you get out of Ms. Jackson's kitchen. I have other crises to attend to. By the way, Lieutenant Thompson," he said, looking straight over the frowning Campbell's head, "good-looking pies."

"Thank you, sir," she said.

"I expect to see you up on the bridge in about, oh, ten minutes. We're about to enter into our new system. I know you wouldn't want to miss a moment."

"Yes, sir!" Thompson rushed to the sink and started washing her hands.

"Thank you," Betty Jackson said in a low voice, following Holcomb out the door. He pulled her arm through his and squeezed her hand. "I didn't mean to start a holy war over turkey and stuffing. My tongue runs away with me, I have to admit."

"Don't mention it," Holcomb said. "I have to say I will be glad when all this is over. It's almost more trouble than having everyone whispering behind my back."

"A lot of that was my fault," Jackson said. "I am sorry. I never meant to undermine your authority. I was just trying to do my job."

"Which you did very well," Holcomb said, sincerely. "Just get the rest of those turkeys into a recognizable shape. I'm a leg man myself."

"Good!" she said, smiling sweetly, eyeing him up and down until he could feel her gaze brush his bare skin. "I will make sure there are lots of drumsticks. I owe you a lot for your support, Captain. Thank you."

"Call me Dan," Holcomb said, feeling his throat constrict like a shy teenager's. If he'd been any closer to puberty his name would have come out as a squeak. Her long lashes flickered flirtatiously.

"I'm Betty, Dan. You know, in my personal luggage I brought along some very good wine. When all this is over, let's go back to my quarters and crack open a bottle. We'll need it by the time this feast comes off." She looked up at him, her lovely eyes laughing. Without quite thinking about it, Holcomb bent down and gave her a peck on the cheek. She turned her head so their lips met. Hers were so warm. Holcomb's skin suddenly felt prickly-sensitive all over, his mouth the most sensitive of all. When he drew back from the kiss, he felt his heart pounding in his chest like one of the drive engines.

"Betty Jackson, will you marry me?" he said, almost breathlessly.

She grinned. "After *my* term as governor." He grinned back. She slipped through the door of the Biochem lab and stood with one hand on each side of the frame. The fabric of her blue shipsuit strained across her breasts, and Holcomb found himself staring. "Say, does that fancy chair of yours recline all the way?"

"All the way," Holcomb said, letting each word drop as slowly as honey, raising his eyes to hers. The door of the galley slid shut. It cut off the sight of her wicked grin. He whistled all the way up to the bridge.

O O O

On the day of the feast, Holcomb felt every eye on him as he appeared in the door of the rec hall. He wore his best dress uniform, pure white with blue piping and gold flashes on shoulders and wrists. Snapping a formal salute to the assemblage, he took off his hat and entered. Commander Campbell himself, crisp and neat in his dress whites, came over to usher the captain to the head of a twenty-meter table set with a gorgeous cascading arrangement of tan and orange leaves. A papier-mâché pumpkin hung overhead, streaming with vines and green leaves that festooned the ceiling like streamers. Colwabe's people had done a fabulous job. Holcomb felt the décor matched the momentous but joyous nature of the occasion. Electric candles glistened on the sideboard among decorations made of wood, yarn, clay, cloth, anything that people had that they wanted to donate to the effort. Hundreds of people had participated to make this feast a success. They *wanted* to belong to a community. All they needed was a cause to rally behind, and they would cooperate beyond anyone's wildest dream. He, and they, had relearned that fact over the last few days.

The turkeys, now coated in a dark, golden-brown glaze that exactly resembled roasted skin were brought out on trays decorated with leaves, and bedecked with jewel-like yams and carrots that looked almost good enough to be real. He chalked up mental kudos to Lieutenant Riga and his hobby, and the determination of the Biochem techs to achieve verisimilitude. The green beans could have been plucked off a vine that morning, instead of being extruded through a plate like twin-lead wire. The bowls of corn gave off a sweet, unmistakable aroma. Everyone had really pulled together for this feast, more than he ever dreamed possible.

The beaming faces meeting Holcomb's gaze made his heart swell with pride in his chest. These were wonderful people. In spite of the years of work he knew were ahead, the colony couldn't be anything but a success with such willing hands and minds like these working together to make it happen. He was proud to be their captain, soon their governor, and one day—he looked across at Betty Jackson, sitting at the opposite end of the table—their peer.

Very ceremoniously, Campbell dished onto his plate a teaspoonful of dark meat, his piece of the real turkey. To Holcomb, it meant more than a tie to the ancient celebration; it was the result of his first successful act as captain. Betty held up a glass to him with her eyebrows raised, offering him the victory and reminding him of her promise, for later. Holcomb smiled back, clasped his hands together and bowed his head over his plate. The entire room fell silent.

"For what we are about to receive," he said, "may we be *truly* thankful."

And he heard her voice loud and clear, even from the other end of a twenty meter table. "Amen."

Holcomb waited in delightful anticipation as Campbell's people came around to carve the soy turkeys into slices, accompanying each plateful with a deferential mutter describing the symbolism of every course on the plate. Each represented the past and the future in one. Holcomb was satisfied.

The future was going to be fun.

CHRISTMAS

The Revenge of Chatty Cathy

"Her name's Chatty Cathy," Perinda's mother, Cherille, told her, handing her the big, brown paper bag. "I wanted one just exactly like her when I was a little girl like you are now. You ought to be lucky you have her."

Perinda stuck out her lip, knowing she didn't look much like a fully-grown up seven-year-old at the moment. She crossed her arms and sat back in the worn rear seat of the ancient, gold Buick. She had had to sit out in the cold on this miserable, dim day, while her mother went in without her, and she didn't get to choose her own birthday present. Having an early December birthday was the pits. All the good stuff was bought already for other children's Christmas presents.

"I don't want an old white doll with brown hair from some resale store. I want a Bratz doll with maybe a motorcycle and an iPod. And some outfits."

"Well, I want the moon," Cherille said, climbing into the driver's seat and looking back over her shoulder. "We're both just about as likely to get what we want. I wish I could shop in Bloomingdale's for you, but we can't afford it. Baby, you have just got to learn how to be happy with what you've got. Take it or I'll take it back. You decide."

"Well . . ."

The girl studied the box in her arms. The doll was kind of pretty. Her hair was the color of chocolate. She liked chocolate. And the eyes were blue, really pretty, with long eyelashes. When she tilted the big doll backwards, the eyes closed. That was kind of cool. Bratz dolls' eyes didn't close. They were painted on. Still, this doll had on the oldest, most moldiest of outfits. It was a red dress with a petticoat, like Perinda wore to church on Sunday. But Chatty Cathy had an interesting face. It wasn't too pretty, and the big blue eyes looked like they had some brains behind them. But what was Perinda thinking? It was just a doll. Dolls were plastic. They didn't have brains.

"It's nice." She knew she sounded half-hearted, but it was hard to make her expectations climb down to reality. The doll looked up at her hopefully.

"Try the pull-string," Cherille said.

Perinda hooked her finger into the plastic loop and pulled it. It drew a string out of Chatty Cathy's back about a foot. When Perinda let it go, a high-pitched voice cooed.

"I love you."

"See?" Cherille beamed. "Isn't that cute?"

Perinda would have had her fingers cut off with a plastic picnic knife than agreed with her mother out loud, but she did think it was kind of cute. "I guess." She tried the string again.

"Will you play with me?"

"Go on, honey, take her out of the package."

Reluctantly, the girl pulled open the flap on top of the box and eased out the long card out to which Chatty Cathy was attached with plastic bands. She undid the ties in the back of the cardboard. The doll slid down so she was sitting in Perinda's lap. Unwittingly, the girl's arms slid around her and held her tightly. It felt right to hug the doll. She felt a charge like electricity, like she'd been waiting a long time to find something this special. She hugged her again, deeply content. Chatty Cathy's big blue eyes blinked up at her.

"You're my best friend," Chatty Cathy said. And she meant it. How long had she been waiting on that dusty shelf, hoping for a real live girl to be friends with her? Years and years had come and gone. Once in a while the man in the shop had taken her down to be examined by various shoppers in search of a birthday or Christmas present. They had pulled her string and listened to her talk. Each and every one had smiled politely and turned away. The man had put her back on the high shelf, behind the fading teddy bears and the plastic Fisher-Price train. After many years, a new manager lowered her price. That did it. This was the moment she had hoped for since the day she had been placed in her box back at the factory. She had been ready to be a friend and confidant. Her miniature record player was in pristine shape. Her dress was neatly pressed, her hair coiffed, and the bloom on her cheeks and lips just the right shade of pink to look like a healthy human girl. She tweaked her smile to be just a little brighter, and saw an answering expression from Perinda. This was the right girl. She was very special. They were going to be good friends, now and forever. She'd do anything to make Perinda happy.

"Isn't that nice?" Cherille asked, as she pulled away from the curb. "Happy birthday, honey."

"Thank you, mama," Chatty Cathy said, a little bumpily.

"Thank you, mama," Perinda echoed. She lifted her hand to pull the string again, then dropped it. It seemed as though the doll talked by itself. That was kind of awesome.

"My name is Cathy. What's yours?"

"I'm Perinda," the girl said, before she realized she was talking with a doll.

"That's pretty. You're pretty," the squeaky voice said.

Perinda pulled at one of her multiple braids self-consciously. "No, I'm not."

"Brown eyes are beautiful."

"Well, thanks."

"You're welcome. You have a nice nose, too."

"It turns up too much."

"Noses should turn up."

Perinda laughed.

"Honey, it sounds like you like your Chatty Cathy."

"She says a lot of things," Perinda said, a little more enthusiastically. "I didn't know they talked so much."

"Where do we live? Are we going there now?"

Cherille's eyes in the mirror looked doubtful. "I never heard of them saying *that* before."

"I'm sorry," Chatty Cathy said, in a doleful voice. "I don't mean to be nosy."

"It's okay," Perinda said, cradling the doll. It made her feel warm and happy to hug her. "Mama, you hurt her feelings."

"Well, I didn't mean to," Cherille said, amused. "I'm sorry, Chatty Cathy."

"I'm happy. Are you happy?"

Perinda thought about it for a moment. "Yeah, I guess. Yeah."

Cherille relaxed in her seat. She had known that her daughter was going to be a little disappointed at getting yet another birthday present from the resale shop, but she seemed to be cheering up. Chatty Cathy was a big success. Who'd have known it had such a sophisticated talk-box for such an old toy? No wonder it had been so expensive back in the 70s. It must use a prototype of artificial intelligence. It was still pretty costly, even in the resale shop. But it was worth every penny to see her daughter's smile as she talked with the doll on her lap. She hadn't been smiling much lately. Their neighborhood had gotten dangerous enough over the last few months that mothers were keeping their kids upstairs in their apartments after school instead of letting them loose in the playground. Perinda, the only one in her grade in their building, had been very lonesome lately. Sounded like she had a new friend, even if it was a toy.

"How old are you?" Chatty Cathy wanted to know.

"I'm seven. Tomorrow."

"Happy birthday!"

"Well, not yet," Perinda said, sheepishly. "Tomorrow."

"I'll say it again tomorrow. I promise. I love you."

"Well, I love you, too," Perinda replied. She hugged the doll. It felt as if the doll hugged back. Even if it was just her imagination, it felt nice.

Cherille was so engaged by the conversation going on in the back seat that she wasn't paying a lot of attention to traffic. A car horn honking brought her back to reality. She jammed on the brakes, and ground to a halt just inches from the fender of a fancy dark blue BMW, driven by a white man in a North Face jacket. Cherille tried to look apologetic. He gave her the finger, and zoomed through the intersection just before the light changed. She shook her head and took a right into the grocery store parking lot.

There were no spaces. She crept out and around to the right again, into the alley, where sometimes there was room to park illegally between the dumpsters. It was nearly dark, but she managed to get the car in underneath a fire escape without scraping anything.

"Now, I'm just going to get some milk and some cereal," Cherille said, turning around to Perinda. "You two stay here and behave yourselves. All right?" She shoved open the door with her elbow.

That was when she felt the cold ring of a gun's barrel touch her temple. She slewed her eyes leftward to the cold, dark eyes of the man holding it. He wore a leather jacket over a filthy green hooded sweatshirt. He couldn't have been more than eighteen. Cherille's heart pounded, almost choking her.

"You get out right now, and nothing's gonna happen to ya," he said.

Another man stepped out of the shadows. About thirty years of age, he had pouches beneath his hazel eyes that made him look angry. Cherille tried to drag her purse out unobtrusively with her.

"Leave it!"

Cherille pointed, careful not to move her head. The round barrel of the gun was ice-cold against her skin. "But I've got to get ..."

"Move your ass out! Now!"

"You got to let me get my ..." The men grabbed her by the arms. They yanked her away from the car and threw her into the heaps of snow plowed up around the Dumpster. Before she could scramble up, the men leaped into the car and roared away down the alley.

Heedless of the cold and wet, Cherille crawled, then ran after her disappearing car. "My baby! Come back with my baby!"

O O O

The two men cackled and exchanged high hand-slaps. "That was too easy!" the hazel-eyed man said. "You dog, Riff! We sell this, and we can be floatin'."

The youth in the hoodie grinned and leaned over the steering wheel. He aimed the old Buick's headlights straight at an old woman with a cane who was trying to cross the street at a stop sign. Her face went slack with alarm, and she hobbled as fast as she could out of their way. To their glee, she slipped in the gutter and went down on her knees. "You got the gun, you got the world, Paulie. Hey, any money in that purse?"

Paulie turned out the cheap leather bag. "About three dollars. Crap."

"Tough luck. We got the car anyhow."

They zipped through the narrow streets, cutting down alleys and under overpasses. The chop-shop that didn't ask questions was about five miles to the south. With the proceeds from even an elderly car, the two could afford enough crack to keep them high for a few days. The fix they'd gotten the day before was wearing off. Paulie was starting to feel itchy and tense. He needed more, and soon.

They screeched to a halt at a stop sign facing an oncoming patrol car, and sat virtuously waiting for it to cross ahead of them.

"You want me to wave to the cop?" Riff asked.

"Stop it, dammit," Paulie said, scratching his ribs uncomfortably.

As soon as the police car was safely past, Riff stomped on the accelerator and flattened them against the seats. "Whee-hew!"

The men went on congratulating themselves on a successful carjacking, and how easy it was to scare ordinary people into giving up their possessions.

"Hey, I don't care what people got, as long as when I want it, I get it, and they don't have it no longer," Riff said.

A tiny voice interrupted them. "I want my mommy."

Riff jammed his foot down on the brake, bringing the Buick to a halt mid-block, causing a delivery van to roll within inches of the rear bumper. The van laid on its horn. Riff automatically thrust his middle finger up out of the window. He turned to look into the darkened rear seat. "What the hell is that?"

Paulie gawked. "It's a kid. A girl."

The little girl trembled, her big brown eyes huge with fear. She pushed herself as far back into the seat as she could. The men glared at her. She managed to get out another sentence. "I want … my mommy."

"Oh, *shit*!" Paulie said.

"We gotta get rid of her," Riff said. He hit the gas again, and turned a few corners, until they were in a street with several derelict houses with overgrown yards. "There." He pointed to an empty lot on the right, where the acid glare from the streetlights left a deep shadow. "Push her out."

"What?"

"Right there. Do it!"

Paulie couldn't think of a better solution to the problem of compounding kidnapping on top of carjacking. As soon as the Buick slid into the curb, he sprang out, yanked open the back door, and pulled the protesting girl out by one arm. He flung her away from him. She landed in the gray-stained snow and rolled over and over. He jumped back in, and Riff peeled away. He glanced behind him. The kid just lay there where she fell, staring after them with her big, brown eyes. She looked forlorn and lost, covered with the dirty snow. Paulie felt bad, but he didn't want no hassles with no kid.

"All right," Riff said, clutching his forehead with one hand. The withdrawal was starting to hit him, too. "That is handled. We gotta get to Buzzy's. I need my fix."

"That was *mean*."

"Shut up." Riff screeched to a halt again. "Dammit, is there another kid in this car?"

Paulie looked in the back seat. "Yeah," he said, grabbing it by the arm. "No, it's a doll. A new doll. Box is right in the corner."

"Bro, toss it out the door after the kid!"

Paulie retrieved the box and inspected it. "No, man, this one's worth money! It's a Chatty Cathy doll. It's vintage. If it's mint, it can be worth bucks. There's a collector store up on the north side. We can go and score some real money for this."

Riff stared at him. "What, you kidding?"

Paulie was serious. He held the little figure up for his friend's inspection. "Nah, man. I saw it on TV, doll once sold for twenty gees on eBay. I could use some of that."

Riff studied the doll with distaste. "Man up north ain't gonna give us no twenty gees."

"Yeah, but he'll give us what he got. It's new. Kid didn't have a chance to mess it up. Dumb kid, didn't know what kind of a gold mine she was sittin' on."

"That's my mama you're talking about," Cathy said, indignantly.

The two men looked at one another. "Did you pull that doll's string?"

"Hell, no."

"Take me back to my mama."

"Aw, come on!" Riff groaned. "That bull make my head ache. Tear her voice box out."

"No!" Paulie said, throwing a protective hand over the doll's body. "It could ruin her value. We gotta keep her intact until we get to the store."

"You're thieves. You're mean to steal a doll away from a nice girl. She never hurt you."

Riff grabbed the side of his head. The desperation was making his head spin. "I don't know if I can take it! Shut her up!"

Paulie picked up the doll and shoved her into the cardboard box. Her hair and skirt got messed up. He tried to shove his hand down into the box to straighten them. It didn't fit.

"You shouldn't use drugs," Cathy observed. "They make your hands shake. You forgot the plastic ties. I'll slide right to the bottom."

Paulie slid Cathy out and tried again. That time he got the skirt hem to keep from riding up, but the hair got flattened on one side and fluffed on the other.

"I bet your mothers are very ashamed that their sons are thieves," Cathy said, her voice not interrupted at all by the cellophane window of her box. "How would you feel if someone took things away from your mother?"

"My mama been robbed a hundred times," Riff snarled, leaning low over the steering wheel. Cathy was pleased. She was making him think. She could tell he didn't like to think. She pressed a little harder.

"Why don't you protect her instead of picking on other people's mothers? Where were you the last time she was robbed?"

"Where the hell were *you*?" Riff countered angrily.

"In Snider's Discount Store on North Broadway," Cathy said at once. There was no reason not to tell them the truth. "Waiting for my mama to come and get me. But I bet you could have helped your mother. Why didn't you?"

Riff couldn't take that much introspection.

"Bro, tear her head off! I don't want to hear her voice one more second!"

Paulie cradled the big pink box protectively in his arms. "Riff, if we damage her, we won't get no money!"

"Yeah, money. Gotta have money. Right now." Riff stared out of the windshield. The streetlights were blurring into big stars of light, obscuring everything but the red tail lights ahead of him. Drugs. He craved the smooth relaxation of a high. "We'll take it to Mumzir's pawn shop. Yeah. He's pretty close."

"You shouldn't take drugs," Cathy said, as the man in the hoodie steered the car unsteadily. "You can't see well, and your reactions are getting very bad. You almost hit that man walking on the street. He was in a crosswalk, so you were in the wrong. I bet you don't even have a valid driver's license. Does yours say you need glasses? Because you do."

"Shut UP!"

"Look out! You almost hit that man!"

The car swerved as Riff's hands jerked nervously.

"Hey," Paulie said, shrewdly, "I bet we get top dollar for her 'cos she can say all these extra things. On the box it says she can only say eighteen phrases. I know she's said at least twenty."

"Twenty-eight so far," Cathy corrected him.

"That's gotta mean she's really special. And all the cool stuff about your mama."

Riff yanked the gun out of his pocket and leveled it at his partner's nose. "You shut up about my mama. You don't say another word about my mama, or I blow you and the doll all over the city."

Paulie held up his hands in surrender. "Okay, man, okay. Cool. Be cool."

O O O

The small, neat, dark-skinned shop owner held the box in his hands. "Yes, Chatty Cathy. We do not see very many of these in this condition. Very good. He looked up at the two men leaning over his counter. "Thirty dollars. That is what I will give you for her. Because she is such excellent condition."

"Thirty?" Riff sputtered. "Bro, she's gotta be worth three thousand!"

Mumzir clicked his tongue. "I cannot pay three thousand. She is a 1970s vintage doll, all accessories accounted for, original box. On a generous percentage of a value of perhaps one hundred dollars, I will give you … forty."

"But she says all these cool things," Paulie said. "Come on, Chatty Cathy, talk to the man."

The three men looked at the doll. Her big blue eyes regarded them with blank friendliness.

"You must pull her string to make her talk," Mr. Mumzir said, shaking his head scornfully at the stupidity. "It says so right on the carton."

"Hell, no," Riff said. "She was talkin' up a storm in the car. Talk now," he ordered the doll. Mumzir regarded him curiously. "I mean it! What you lookin' at me for? She said things about my mama!"

"I can see that you are high," Mumzir said. "Drugs rot your mind, you know." He pulled the ring on the doll's body.

"Night, night, Mommy," Chatty Cathy said.

"You see, nothing out of the ordinary," Mumzir said, shaking his head. "Forty dollars."

"I want more!" Riff said. He pulled his gun out of his pocket and aimed it at the shop owner. Calmly, Mumzir shook his head.

"You are under video surveillance. Besides, my three brothers have had weapons trained on you since you came in here. Put it away, or I will tell the police when they come to collect your bodies that it was self-defense. We have licenses for our firearms. Do you?"

Riff and Paulie sprang into a back-to-back *Starsky and Hutch* pose, searching the mirrored cases for signs of the other three Mumzirs. Glaring hatred at the shop owner, Riff stuck the gun into his waistband and yanked the front of the hoodie down over it.

"All right," he said, trying to regain his dignity. "Forty dollars, and make it fast."

Mumzir went to a small keypad set in the wall and started to enter numbers.

"I am stolen merchandise," Chatty Cathy said suddenly. "I am stolen merchandise. They stole me. I am stolen merchandise."

Mumzir's hand dropped from the keypad. "What? Is the doll saying the truth?"

"Naw, it's just a recording, bro," Riff said, casually.

"They stole the car they drove here in, too," Cathy continued. "From a nice lady and her little girl. They threw them out of the car and took it."

"Carjacking?" Mumzir's swarthy cheeks paled. Something was strange. Could this be a police sting? "How dare you come in here? I do not receive stolen merchandise from thieves! Get out." He pointed toward the door.

Riff and Paulie thought about arguing the point, but remembered the guns hidden in the walls.

"All right," Riff said, leveling a finger at Mumzir as he backed toward the door. "But I'll be back. Don't you forget it."

"You don't forget what I say," Mumzir said. "Leave before I call the police! Come back when you actually own what you want to sell me."

Paulie snatched up Chatty Cathy and the carton. The two men made as dignified an exit as they could. The security door snapped shut behind them.

"Will you take me back to my mama now?" Chatty Cathy asked. "Please? I am sure she is very scared."

Riff grabbed the box out of Paulie's hands. "I can't take no more of this damned *doll*!" He wrenched open the Buick's bent trunk lid, threw Cathy inside, and slammed it shut. "Get in! We gonna go right to Buzzy's, right now! I gotta have my fix."

It wasn't very dark inside the trunk. Cathy's box had landed face upwards. She could see a few small holes that let in light, and sound. From the compartment of the car, she heard the two men arguing. Their voices sounded faint and hollow. They wouldn't listen to her.

The car lurched away from the curb. Cathy went flying against the rear of the trunk. She had to get back to Perinda. She must take care of her newfound mother.

She could hear the noise of other cars and the sloshy footsteps of people on the sidewalks. Each time the car jerked to a halt, she listened for people approaching.

"Help me!" she shouted, straining her speaker to the maximum. "Please, get me out of this trunk! The men driving are very bad. Help me!"

O O O

Miranda Benitez hoisted her briefcase strap onto her shoulder. The gold car had stopped for the light right in the middle of the crosswalk. Grumbling, she stepped off the curb and angled around the vehicle's rear end, trying to avoid the slush. Her shoes were already wet, and her toes were beginning to freeze.

"Help me!" a tiny voice said. Miranda looked around. "Please, get me out of this trunk! I have to get back to my mama!"

Miranda realized the voice was coming from the car beside her. There was a little girl in there. A kidnapping! She glanced at the driver, and knew she didn't want to mess with him, but she had to help.

"Hang in there, baby," Miranda whispered. "I'll get help."

She took her cell phone out of the pouch hanging from her purse strap and dialed 911. She dashed out of the crosswalk and stood on the opposite curb.

"Yes, I'm sure what I heard. An old Buick, gold color, license plate number 518 HRM. Hurry! She sounds scared."

O O O

"Ah, shit!" Riff said, looking in the rear view mirror at the flashing blue lights. His heart raced. He hoped it wasn't him the cops were following, but the loud hoot of the siren disabused him of the idea. They were only two blocks from Buzzy's! He rolled down the window as the patrol cop approached, and put on a big fat smile. "Can I help you, officer?"

The police sergeant, a burly man with his winter coat buttoned up underneath a jowly double chin, raked Riff and Paulie with a blazing white flashlight beam. "License and registration, please?"

Riff felt his pockets. "Well, I've got 'em somewhere, officer. I'm drivin' on a ticket, okay, bro?" He produced the much folded piece of paper, and held it out with two fingers.

"Registration?"

"Look, it's my mama's car. I don't know where she keeps the registration."

"I see," the cop said, evenly. Riff started to relax. He was buying it. "Would you mind opening your trunk, please?"

Warily, Riff pushed open the door. The cop stood out a little, not turning his back on the two men. He kept them ahead of him as Riff pulled the key out of the ignition and went around to the back. He felt around for the latch, hoping it wasn't in some weird place. He'd kill that bitch if she had some kind of illegal goods in the trunk! Getting him pulled over, when he had priors in his record!

But, no, there was nothing in there except for that damned doll. The cop rocked back on his heels.

"Can we go now?" Riff asked hastily. "I've got an appointment."

"I guess …" the policeman began.

"Help me," the doll said, unexpectedly. "These men stole me from my mama. I want to go back. Please take me to 2534 South Lawndale. It's dark. I bet she's really scared. And cold."

The cop glared at Riff and Paulie, who was trying to edge away onto the curb. "Is this some kind of joke? We got a report from some woman who heard a little girl's voice in the trunk."

"Come on, officer," Riff said, ingratiatingly. He leaned a little closer, but the policeman backed away half a pace. "It's just a doll. It goes off all by itself sometime. It's defective." He slammed his palm down on the box, bursting the cellophane. Paulie let out a gasp and gave Riff a reproachful look. *"What?"*

"That was me, officer," Chatty Cathy said, promptly. "Thank you for stopping. These mean men took my mama's mama's car. They pushed her out into the snow. It was a carjacking. They have a gun. They want to buy drugs. They were about to pawn this car with someone named Buzzy. Have you ever heard of him?"

The officer's eyes widened, but his eyebrows lowered until they met at the bridge of his broad nose. "You bet I've heard of him. Buzzy, huh?"

"It's just a doll!" Riff protested.

By then the police officer had his gun in his hand. "All right, you two. Assume the position. I don't care if the doll's defective or not. I'm going to check into this. Where's that gun?"

"Who says I got one?" Riff asked, turning to face the car. He spread his hands on the trunk lid.

"Right now," the cop said, "I'm gonna believe the doll. Where is it?"

"Waistband," Riff choked out. The cop held him down with an elbow and yanked the pistol out of his jeans front. He did a quick pat-down of both men, then reached for his radio.

"Dispatcher 26, this is 26-32. I need a rundown on, er, an '86 Buick, license number …"

"My head is killing me," moaned Paulie.

O O O

By the time the police sergeant rolled onto the 2500 block of South Lawndale, two other patrol cars were already parked on the grass. A short, broad-faced black woman stood rocking a little girl in her arms. The child's long legs hung limply around her hip, and she had her face hidden in the woman's shoulder. A quartet of officers, one of them a uniformed lieutenant, surrounded them. Cameras with bright white lights were trained on them, and reporters had microphones aimed at their mouths.

"This baby was too scared to talk," the woman was saying, "but I knew she was in trouble. That's when I called you."

The sergeant managed to look dignified as he carried Chatty Cathy over the trampled snow.

"Perinda? Is this your doll?" he asked.

The child raised her head. Her expression of fear and woe changed suddenly as she spotted the doll in his hand. She nodded. The sergeant held it out. The girl reached for it and wrapped it in her arms.

"I love you," Chatty Cathy said at once. Perinda was still too upset to speak, but she squeezed harder and buried her face in the chocolate-colored hair.

The lieutenant gave the sergeant an odd glance. "How'd you know the child's name? We haven't been able to get a word out of her."

The sergeant thought about it for a moment, and realized he didn't want to make a fool of himself in front of the news teams. He'd gotten an earful all the way there, but how could he say his information had come from a 24-inch plastic doll with freckles? "Information received, sir. I located the mother. She was down at the 6th Precinct, making a report." The reporters, hearing another source of hot information for their breaking news story, stuck the microphones in his face. The lieutenant looked peeved, but he gave the sergeant a nod to go on. "She's frantic but she's okay. She'll be here any moment. We've arrested two men for an armed carjacking. Down behind the food store on 35th Street. Couple of junkies looking for a fix. We've also got them for kidnapping and felony theft. They can't hurt this little girl or her mother ever again. We've recovered the car. It's up at the 10th precinct lot."

The reporters burst into a cacophony of questions. The sergeant and lieutenant did their best to answer them over the head of the woman who had taken in the little girl abandoned on the street.

"… And she is reunited with her precious doll just in time for her very special seventh birthday," one of the on-air reporters told her camera sincerely. "Birthday wishes for this brave little girl can be sent to the Channel Four website. The address is on the bottom of the screen."

"You'll be all right now," Chatty Cathy confided to Perinda. "Carjacking carries a mandatory sentence. Those two scary men are going to be locked up for years. Your mother will be here soon. Then we can go home. I can't wait to see our home."

"You came back for me," Perinda whispered. "How come you did all that?"

Chatty Cathy fixed her big blue eyes contentedly on Perinda, and felt satisfied to the depths of her cotton stuffing. "Because you're my best friend."

Mistletoe

Rhodri could barely believe the good fortune that the gods had bestowed upon him, and through him, all the people of Llyn. The lean, dark-haired man kept the pure white cloth cradled against his chest under the shelter of his green woolen hood and cloak all the way from the edge of the forest to the center of town. The sharp, crisp, green leaves and white berries of mistletoe had glinted at him from the trunk of an oak along the black scar where lightning had struck it during the autumn rains. Born of fire and collected in just the right way, the leaves and berries would provide powerful protection to the townsfolk. Despite the fresh, ankle-deep snow that slickly coated the stone cobbles of the streets and chilled his feet through his wooden-soled leather boots and thick knitted socks, he had run all the way back to the chief druid's cottage, to bring him out to see the miracle. Alas, Gryffydd was not at home. Instead of waiting, Rhodri decided to surprise him. He took a piece of clean linen from Gryffydd's press and the golden sickle from the druid's chest of books and mystical devices. Rhodri praised the gods that he knew the correct prayers to say while harvesting a few sprigs of the mistletoe, although he was almost certain to be chided by Gryffydd for doing the ritual himself at all. He was but a bard, not yet a full initiate, though he had recently been allowed to do some small charms and healings in the company of an experienced ovate, he sang the chants during their meetings, and he joined the three hundred druids at the Powys council when a grave decision was to be made.

The moon would be full at week's end, when they marked the winter solstice, also known as the second Gathering Day. At that time, the druids would collect the parasitic plant from all parts of the forest and take it to the grove, where it would be blessed by the entire circle of druids and the pure silver light of the moon herself, then either put to use as protection, medicine or part of spells to benefit the people of Llyn. With sun's light beginning again to wax from that day, the power of the rituals they performed would be all the greater.

The mistletoe had not lost its virtue through his inexpert handling, thank all gods. He could feel the incredible power of the vine right through the cloth. It was said that the mistletoe had magnetic properties as well as magic. Indeed, it felt as though it was pulling his heart almost out of his lean chest. Oh, Gryffydd must rejoice! Rhodri began to compose a poem in the honor of the sacred plant. He hummed measures, trying this phrase and that in his warm tenor voice.

"Shall I fetch your harp, master?" Llew panted. The servant, a leggy boy rising twelve, with a shock of crisp black hair and dark blue eyes like sunlight reflected in a peat-logged pool, ran to come up alongside him. Naturally, he had not been permitted to touch neither sickle nor plant, but had followed Rhodri into the woods, dagger drawn, to protect them both in case of attack from bandits or animals. Now that they were among houses and shops, he sheathed it again. The few passersby nodded their greetings to the two men. Rhodri could smell the mouth-watering aroma of fresh-baked bread steaming up from the bundle wrapped well against the cold of the day in the arms of Mistress Islwyn, wife of Huw the Dyer.

"Nay," Rhodri said, grinning at the boy. "As soon as we're home again, there'll be time for music! After we take this to Gryffydd's home, run along ahead of me and make sure the fire's stirred up. You stay there." He glanced at the lad's red nose and the hint of water in his eyes. He wished he could take a pinch of the sacred vine to treat Llew's oncoming ague, but until it was blessed he didn't like to call upon its powers. "Crush some rosemary and onion together and take it in wine."

"I am all right, master," Llew said, sheepishly. Rhodri smiled. At least the boy was well wrapped up in good woolen clothes; being the apprentice to a tailor had some perquisites. Those studying to join the grove were supposed to be immune from unhealthy humors, but Rhodri knew it was an ideal that poor mankind could never reach. He was glad that the boy and others like him were so willing to risk themselves to gain wisdom. With the advent of the Saxons on the very shores of sacred Mona and the great outspreading of the church of the Christ, the druids and others who worshiped the gods of nature were becoming more threatened every day. Instead of living in isolated cottages to study magic and contemplate the gods, all of the druids but the Archdruids in Mona and Pontypridd had taken jobs and professions that suited their skills. Llew had come to Rhodri as both a postulant to the grove and an apprentice tailor.

As they came into Llyn's market square, Llew glanced up, and his face cracked into a broad smile, showing the gap on the side where the boy had lost a tooth. "There's Mistress Bronwen coming this way."

Rhodri spotted the plump woman heading toward them. Back when he'd been drifting and foolish, he had joined with her more than once in the May Day dancing and private celebration on beds of dried leaves in the forests. Now they were both rising thirty. As a devotee to the grove, he had never married. Bronwen had been widowed five years before, leaving her with four children that she supported with her skills as a brewster. She was still beautiful, and would be until the day the gods folded her into their bosom. Rhodri regretted that their separate paths could no longer converge. He had set his feet upon the path of scholarship and purity, and she had risen to the high priestesshood of the witches' coven. Both their groves were steeped in their own mysteries, though it was a fairly open secret among the people of Llyn that they existed. The overlord of Wales, King Hywel Dda, was nominally a Christian, but he treated the wise ones who practiced the old ways with respect. He believed in magic, as it had kept him safe against the interlopers from overseas. He used power from wherever it arose, unlike the Archbishop of Canterbury and his priests and monks, who disbelieved in anything that did not come from their Christ.

"Rhodri," she called to him, waving a small, plump hand. Even in a modest, dark blue bliaut with a white head rail that covered her thick, dark soft hair, the undulations of her soft, curving body invited his own. He felt the old urges arising in him. The quickening of breath, the pounding of his heart in his own ears, the swelling of his nether member were all welcome to him, proving he was alive. He knew, as she did, that he had sacrificed his bodily comfort for the sake of magic and scholarship. He just couldn't help but stare at her. The marvel of her, being able to glide over the snow as though she sailed on a pond! "And you're looking well! Where have you been? And what's there, now? Another measure of cloth for the cutting?" She nodded toward the bundle in his arms.

As she was a fellow celebrant, there was no harm in letting her see. He lowered his hands and spread the linen out over them. The gold glint of the plant with its gleaming white berries took what sad, thin sunshine peeked out between the heavy clouds and turned it into a warm glow. Bronwen's eyebrows rose to the edge of her veil.

"That is a powerful herb you have there, my brother," she said. "I can feel the lightning in it. Did it grow on that great oak thirty paces beyond the fork in the Aberystwyth crossroads?"

"It did," he said. "I did not see this mistletoe before, but the wind we had two nights ago seems to have cracked away the twigs hiding it from view. It wasn't there on Gathering Day at the summer solstice, so I believe the gods placed it there during the rains in August."

"That would be enough to draw the crab from the chest of old Gareth," Bronwen said, holding her hands above the cluster and rubbing them together as if warmed by its fire. "It's worth a try."

"I shall ask Master Gryffydd," Rhodri said, with respect. She had always been more skilled an herbalist than he. He tilted his head back in the direction of his servant. "And a little for my *bach*, Llew. The cold has gotten into him. The power in this will drive it out."

"Master!" Llew's cry of warning came a moment too late.

"Pagan nonsense! God's will heals the sick, not your pretense of magic!"

A blow struck Rhodri's hands from below. The cloth and its precious contents went flying. He scrambled to retrieve them, as more strokes rained down on his back. His upper arm caught hot fire where the stick struck it. Instead of picking up the mistletoe, his hands grasped sodden snow.

He twisted to avoid his assailant, and threw the clumps of wet slush in the direction from which the blows had come. Another hard whack took him in the wrist. The agony rendered his fingers numb. He gawked in horror. The attacker was Father Nudd. The gaunt Christian priest, dressed in heavy black wool gown and hood, kept striking at him with his black staff. The silver cross at its top radiated cold disapproval.

"Back to your cloth, tailor!" he shouted. "Leave the weeds for the cattle! These unholy plants have no more power than a stone."

Rhodri held his arms up, but only to defend himself. It was ill in the eyes of the gods to strike a fellow celebrant; more to the point, it was against the king's law to hit a priest of the Christ. Worse yet, Nudd was not alone. More sons of Eire, dressed in brown wool, their heads shaved to show bare crowns to the sky, hulked at Nudd's back, ready to strike with their own staves if Rhodri retaliated. All he could do was dodge out of reach until the priest stopped striking at him. His feet slipped on the wet cobbles, just as the staff descended again with a *whack!* To his shame, a few of the women selling winter apples and pots of beer came over to see what was going on.

"Leave me be, Nudd!" he said, doing his best to keep his own temper. "The gods have plans for us all."

"Only one God rules all," Nudd boomed. By then, even he realized he had drawn a crowd from the nearby market stalls. The townsfolk's breath rose up in white clouds as they whispered among themselves. Too late, Nudd pulled himself together and straightened his narrow back.

"God will punish you for your savage ways!" he snarled. His ascetic countenance, with its thin, pinched nose and flared nostrils, resembled the pale illuminations painted on the inside of the wooden church at the top of the road. He looked as though he still wanted to strike out. Instead of attacking Rhodri again, he spotted a saucer beside the doorpost of the baker. It was filled with milk for the elves, a custom that went back farther than doorposts and saucers, to bring luck to the owner of the house. Nudd raised his staff high with both hands and brought the end crashing down in the center of the dish. It shattered into five pieces, sending milk splattering in every direction.

"Anathema!" he declared, aiming a bony finger at each of the folk who had gathered to watch. "These pagan ways are evil! Turn away from them or God will turn his countenance from you!"

He stormed away, his monks in his wake. The others went back to their interrupted bargains, murmuring low among themselves. A couple of stray cats crept over to lap up the milk before it seeped away in between the icy cobblestones.

"That's a frustrated man," Bronwen said, watching the Christians retreat.

"That's an angry man," Rhodri said, pulling up his sleeves to examine his bruises. He felt like the dish, split into pieces. Though his slender fingers ached, none of them was broken. The marks on his forearms were red, but the place where Nudd had struck his wrist was already rising purple. His ribs ached as though he had fallen off a cliff and tumbled over rocks. Luckily, nothing was really badly injured. "His soul can't be pleasing to his god." It was difficult to regain his composure, but he forced himself to remember that Druid lore warned that heat melted away intelligence. A clear head meant a softly-beating heart, the seat of wisdom. In spite of his efforts, the pain made his temper flare again.

Bronwen set a gentle hand on his arm and murmured soft words. A warm red glow that only he or another initiate would be able to see rose from her fingers. He felt a slight shock as it sank into his flesh. Wiccan healing was different than druidic spells but, if Rhodri was honest, just as effective. He let out a breath as the pain dissolved away. Rhodri met her eyes and smiled for thanks.

"He needs a woman so badly that it hurts," Bronwen said, shrugging in the direction of the departed priest. "He's always wanted me, but I'd never take a man so angry. It would be bad for the magic, to be sure, but it would also injure both of us."

Rhodri shook his head. For all they proclaimed celibacy, humility, and poverty, the Christian religious were seldom any of the three. Some of them had women who lived with them, others visited women, and even men. Poverty, when they had clothes finer than the townsfolk who ran businesses? Not a chance. And humility, none at all.

"Is there any who would touch him? He wields power, whether or not he will acknowledge it. It could burn a decent person to death."

Bronwen smiled, a wicked twinkle in her eyes. "Mistress Wynedd would risk it, in a heartbeat." She named the headman's daughter, a pretty girl with long tresses of yellow hair, who was as yet unmarried though her younger sister was handfast to their father's kinsman. "Master Huw wouldn't mind, to be sure. He'd give her the sun and moon if it would make her happy."

"If only we could put them together," Rhodri said, mischief matching her own in his heart. "But that would mean the breaking of his vows. And yours as well as mine, to do no harm. I can't let you participate in such a prank."

"Ah, well," she said, with an exaggerated sigh that heaved her generous bosom up and down. "It was but a moment's notion, and would solve so many problems all at once. The girl's been after me for a love philter, but I won't make her one."

"For him?" Rhodri asked in astonishment.

"For him," Bronwen said, dimpling.

"Well, there's no understanding taste, is there?"

"None at all, or would I still fancy you?" She glanced around, and spotted the abused mistletoe against the wall of the dyer's shop. She picked it up and offered it to Rhodri. He held his hands up, away from the plant. It had lost a good deal of its luster.

"It's of no use to the grove now that it has touched the ground." He hesitated, with regret. She would understand the mysteries well, but he was oath-bound not to reveal them to an outsider from the Druidic rites. "I can tell you no more than that."

She tucked it into the pouch at her belt. "Ah, waste not, want not. The gods be with you, Rhodri."

"And with you, Mistress Bronwen."

O O O

The strings of his lap harp jangled under his fingertips. Rhodri had pulled his backless wooden stool just far enough from the fire to protect the instrument from the heat. The smoke, as stirred up as his emotions, swirled around the low room instead of lifting toward the smoke hole in the slate-tiled roof. He rose, lit a cluster of dried leaves from the blaze, and held it near the ceiling until the fumes followed it, like sheep after their wether.

His fellow druids, eleven in number, sat around the fire pit, their woolen hoods thrown back thanks to the warmth. Master Gryffydd sat in the best chair, an oak seat carved in the Roman fashion, though with claws for feet and fantastic beasts painted and incised on every inch of wood in the Celtic manner of ornamentation. His long gray beard lay upon his breast like a grand pectoral of silver. Llew served all of them wine, but he kept his eye especially upon the level in the chief druid's cup. They were there to discuss the coming Solstice ritual, but no one could keep off the topic of the priest's assault upon Rhodri.

"So," Gryffydd asked after the bard had told his tale, "what manner of recompense do you require for the brutal attack Nudd made upon you? Will you ask that he be brought before the tribunal? His highness the king will visit here a few days after the mass of the Christ so the people can drink his health. We have other matters to which we shall need to draw his attention. He struck you in front of witnesses."

Rhodri pulled his small harp into his lap once more, and plucked a threnody from the thin horsehair strings. The plaintive sound echoed his thoughts.

"My bruises are healing, thanks to Mistress Bronwen," the bard said, fighting down his immediate impulse to demand retribution. If he ever wanted to take the next step and be admitted to the inner grove of full druids, he had to let such things pass. He took a deep breath. "I'm more offended on behalf of the mistletoe. He cast down some of our most sacred plant. Its power was wasted."

"Aye," said old Einar, his winter-white brows jutting out over a clifflike nose. "That lack of respect must be noted."

The others chimed in their agreement. Gryffydd held up his hand.

"It has been noted. But to rebalance his crime against the mistletoe, and against you as well, he must feel the power of it."

"In what way, master?" Rhodri asked, concerned that such rebalancing was outside his ability.

"In whatever way fate permits. It need not be force where force was offered. There are so many means of exacting divine justice. The gods love laughter as much as they value reverence. Otherwise, why would they have structured our bodies in such haphazard fashion? When one beholds a stag, majesty and power are evident in the way it springs, the way it carries its head, the antlers that show the masculine anima. Look at men, poor things that we are. We come in all sizes and shapes, and our bodies do not reflect the wisdom or strength of our souls. If your body matched your will and nobility, you would have the stature of a giant, for refusing to call the priest into tribunal."

"But, master," Einar protested, "what about the mistletoe?"

Gryffydd smiled, his long, gray mustache lifting at the corners of his mouth. "If the mistletoe was offended, then it must be allowed to take its own vengeance upon the priest, if it will. Otherwise, none of us will raise our hand against him. Are we in agreement?" He turned his keen gaze upon them all until they nodded. "Very well. Let us discuss the coming solstice, when we welcome the return of the sun. Then let us discuss our ritual for the night. It will be a rare and beautiful confluence, the moon full on the very night of the solstice. All the gods will be among us. It will be a night of great power, and thanks to our brother Rhodri's sharp eyes, we shall have mistletoe born of the oak and the lightning to bless us in the coming seasons."

Rhodri let out his breath slowly. He was satisfied, and Gryffydd had seen him exercise restraint. The turn of the year toward growing light was a time to let go of old grudges and move toward purity and reason.

O O O

That Saturday night, under the full moon, the druids in their white woolen robes and crowns of holly leaves sacrificed the white bull of prophecy beneath the lightning-struck oak tree. The portents for the year ahead that they read in his blood were better than any of them dared hope. The harvests would be rich, the flocks were destined to increase well, and no loss was foreseen among the children that would be born to the women of the village.

The youngest of the druid caste, Tamsin, scaled the mighty tree and cut away all the gold stems and leaves and white berries of the gift from the gods as Rhodri in his clear tenor voice sang the prayers. The plant was bursting with power, shooting miniature green lightning bolts in every direction. Gryffydd looked decades younger in their light. He led the chanting as all twelve initiates held their right hands over the plants, asking for the gods' blessings on the mistletoe. Those of the outer grove peered over their shoulders at the marvel. The shining berries gleamed like the full moon overhead.

"Let protection, wisdom, fertility, prosperity, and health be the gifts the gods give to us this year," the chief druid intoned.

"So mote it be," the entire grove responded.

"And let the energy we raise here tonight be within us, now and forever." Gryffydd drew in a deep breath. The others followed suit. Rhodri felt as though he was buoyed up by the moonlight, the smell of bull's blood, and the lightning. When the senior druid spoke again, his voice was full of power. "We will share this gift with all of the people of Llyn. Such is our vow."

"So mote it be," the whole grove responded. Rhodri thought that he could hear other voices in the distance: female voices, chanting the same words. He smiled to himself. Bronwen and her circle were celebrating the sabbat, too.

The morning following the solstice celebration, Rhodri still felt as though he was walking upon clouds rimmed with fire. In a pouch of purest white cloth, he had sprigs of the mistletoe, still expelling tiny bolts of green fire. He and his brothers of the grove were abroad to distribute the blessing to everyone. Llew carried a basket with a ball of twine and hooks to hang the gifts up above the door of every house.

The townsfolk knew what he was about. Most of them met him at the door as he approached.

"Gods' grace upon you, Rhodri Tailor," Mistress Norda said.

"Gods be with you, too," Rhodri replied. He offered a branch of mistletoe to her. "Grant you and your family prosperity and fertility throughout this year."

"The gods be thanked," Norda said. She had three sons but desperately wanted a daughter. "My husband is getting firewood. Would you affix it over the door?" She smiled broadly. "I want to greet him properly when he returns."

"My pleasure," Rhodri said. Llew unspooled two lengths of string and handed them over one at a time. As Rhodri tied the branch over the low lintel, he felt the bolts of power flow into the framework of the house, settling into the earth and surrounding the small building with the strength of oak.

"Rhodri!" He heard footsteps squelching through the mud and turned to see Bronwen hurrying toward him. "Come quick. Nudd has gone mad."

Rhodri followed her through the narrow lane that passed between the butcher's house and the candlemaker's.

"He came to visit this morning, no doubt to chide me for missing prayers, as if I was going to be abroad at dawn after last night, and tore your gift of mistletoe from my doorpost. I only know what happened when I heard the plant cry out."

Indeed, it seemed as though the priest had lost his senses. He ran from house to house, his black skirts flying, grabbing at the mistletoe springs and throwing them to the ground. A monk picked up the discarded branches. On the steps of the small, slate-roofed church, the monks were throwing the mistletoe sprigs on a bonfire. As the flames touched them, they expelled one final burst of brilliant green force, then died. Rhodri felt the loss. It filled him with rage so fierce that he did not recognize himself. They insulted his faith and left the villagers open to ill luck and bad spirits!

"This must be stopped," he said. "Llew, with me!" He took a thin log from beside the door of the nearest house and stalked toward the priest. The boy grabbed a stick and hurried after him.

"That's not the way," Bronwen said, stepping between. She planted her hands on his chest He could feel their heat through his heavy cloak. Her deep blue eyes bored into his. "Please, as you love me, do not strike him down! It will go ill for all. Think of your soul! Any ill you do him will rebound upon you threefold."

Rhodri pulled in a deep breath. He knew the witches' rede. The sacred law was as true for the druids as for them. He dropped the log. It fell to the wet stones with a clatter. Llew took both pieces of wood and set them back on the pile. "Then, what?"

"This is the season for new beginnings," she said. "Let us give Nudd something to rejoice in."

"Bring *him* joy?" Rhodri asked. "How?"

She glanced around. "There!"

The priest was at the edge of the open square opposite the headman's house, which had not yet been gifted. The commotion, of villagers protesting the destruction of the mistletoe and the religious haranguing them, had drawn the curiosity of the chief's house. The door unlatched, but instead of the headman, his yellow-haired daughter peered out. She saw the priest, and her lovely face filled with confusion.

"Her?"

"Her."

"But what about your own vow? 'An it harm none, do what thou wilt'?"

"This will not harm them. It will do them both good. Do you not trust your gods to do what's right? Well, then."

Bronwen bustled to young Wynedd. Rhodri followed, uncertainty warring with hope in his heart.

"What is he doing, Mistress?" the girl asked, in bewilderment, watching the priest storming from house to house.

The witch threw an arm around her shoulders. "Come inside with me, girl." She beamed at the headman, who sat at his table with his morning ale and a round loaf of white wheaten bread. The long room was warm and cozy. Its walls were lined with hand-wrought tapestries, and the air smelled of savory cooking. Master Huw's mother, seated by the hearth, her back straight in spite of her ancient years, nodded to Bronwen, sister to sister. Rhodri's long-held guess that Mistress Mhairi was also of the coven was fairly well confirmed. Llew came in shyly and stood as close to the fire as he dared.

"Good day to you, Mistress Bronwen, Master Bard, boy," Master Huw said heartily. "Are you here to give us the blessing?

"I am," Rhodri said. "But the protection this year may take a turn you have not seen before. Have you noted the chaos going on out in the street?"

"Ach, that madman?" Huw said. He shook his head impatiently. "He was a bright, normal lad. I wish he had kept the wisdom in his head and farmed sheep with his father instead of taking the joy out of everyone else's life."

Bronwen bent to look Wynedd in the eyes. "You have held that wild fellow out there in esteem for some time, have you not?"

The girl's round cheeks reddened. She looked shy to speak before the bard and her father, but her feelings came out all in a rush.

"I do, Mistress Bronwen!"

"Well, then! Let me and Master Rhodri make for you a symbol of hope and fertility for the coming year. We will make this special. Take the gift from your bag, master bard."

Rhodri drew the finest sprig from among the boughs of mistletoe and held it between them. As if it knew what they had planned for it, it erupted in a cascade of tiny green lightnings that lit up the long, dim room. Rhodri willed all power and protection he could summon from sky and root into the golden plant. Bronwen held her hands above and below the bough, without touching it.

"I call earth and water," she said, and warm, red power flowed from her palms into the mistletoe. "Let the power of the gods bestow health, wealth, and joy upon this household on this joyous day of the winter solstice."

"I call air and fire," Rhodri said, smiling at Bronwen. He felt the bond form between them as it once had been. "Let the power of the gods bestow wisdom, fertility, and protection upon this household on this joyous day when the sun returns to the land." The green lightning shot out in all directions, then arrowed inward. Instead of warring, as he feared, the two magics combined, evoking images in colored fire: a rose, a holly wreath, a crown of bright jewels, a sword, and a cup. The images died away as Rhodri sealed the spell. The plant then looked as ordinary as any he had placed around the village. Only those with the sight would be able to see the two forces within suffusing every cell of the mistletoe. He placed it over the lintel just inside the door.

"Thank you, wise … bard, and gracious lady," Huw said. He reached into his belt pouch and put silver into their hands, the value of a gold coin apiece.

Heavy pounding interrupted them. The wooden door flew open, letting in a gust of freezing air.

"Master Huw!" Father Nudd intoned. His black skirts swirled with the wind. His black hood flapped on his shoulders. The long face could not have looked more forbidding or disapproving. "May I enter?"

The headman shot a look at Rhodri as though asking permission. Rhodri took in a deep breath, and nodded.

"Come, and welcome," Huw said.

As the man stepped onto the threshold, the hanging mistletoe brushed his head. Rhodri felt the power of the strong mistletoe take hold. The priest's face changed. He looked up in horror as he saw the sacred plant. He plunged forward, but instead of grabbing the wreath from above the door, he seized Wynedd in his arms and began to kiss her. She squealed, at first in surprise, but then in delight. She put her arms around him and held tight, returning every kiss with all her pent-up longing.

In the very next breath, Nudd realized his terrible error. He pushed at the girl's shoulders, trying to get free. Rhodri glanced at Huw. The headman, instead of looking outraged, was pleased. It meant that the churchman would have to show favor to the family, if for no other reason than to keep the scandal quiet.

Nudd extricated himself, but the magic was too strong. No matter how he tried to extricate himself, his arms stayed wrapped around the girl's body. For the first time in years, he was more man than priest. He kept plunging into the kiss again and again, covering the girl's face and neck with passionate lips. She giggled and her eyes closed in sheer bliss.

Huw smiled broadly.

"Is this a new custom of the church, priest?" he asked. "Kissing under the mistletoe?"

"No! I, uh …" Unable to resist for even a moment, Nudd bent again to his work. Wynedd threw her arms around his neck and cuddled closer against him.

"Well, then, perhaps it should be," the headman declared. "My daughter seems to be enjoying it mightily."

At last, Nudd managed to drag in a breath of air, and glared at Rhodri.

"*You* did this," he growled, before Wynedd dragged his head down again.

"I?" Rhodri asked, watching with growing amusement. "I serve the gods of nature. If this is so unnatural, let her go."

"I … I can't!"

"Can't, or won't?" Huw asked. "My friend the king comes to Llyn on the second day of Christmas. What on Earth shall I tell him and his friend the bishop about this priest?"

"Nothing," Bronwen said. "Look how happy they are. Well, we must take our leave. Good Yule to you, Huw."

Huw gave them a broad wink.

On the threshold, Bronwen took Rhodri's face between her hands and kissed him soundly on the mouth. The bard felt the crackle as though lightning passed between them. He gasped. The witch smiled.

"Have we done ill?" he asked, nodding toward the closed door. Bronwen waved a hand in dismissal.

"Not a whit. That was what Nudd needed. You have given him a proper Yule present. It will save his soul."

"He will break his vows," Rhodri said, feeling the shame Nudd must be experiencing even alongside the joy.

Bronwen shook her head. "Then he will confess the sins and be forgiven. That is their way. In the meanwhile, we will have peace for a time. The girl is happy, and her father is not displeased. You have made all well. Go on and give the rest of your gifts to the village." She glanced toward the fire on the church steps. It had burned down to a few embers. The monks around it looked puzzled when their master did not emerge from the headman's house with another prize.

Rhodri was struck by a dismaying thought. He clutched Bronwen's arm.

"She will surely conceive. The mistletoe never fails. Not with all that power within it."

"Ah, no trouble for all that. It wouldn't be the first priest's brat in these parts, nor the last, and look how many masses the deed will buy for the soul of our worthy headman. Huw has a toe in all our circles."

Rhodri looked down at Bronwen fondly. The power that passed between them was not all due to the mistletoe.

"Ah, my dear," he said. "I owe you a debt."

She gave him a wicked smile that made the dimples in her rosy cheeks indent. "Then you shall pay it. And you can pay it off at midnight tonight, while the moon is still full. I don't want you to become like Nudd. It'll be your Yule gift to me."

He smiled at her. Even Gryffydd would agree that a wise man knew when to withdraw and when to come forward. "It is a debt I will gladly pay, mistress. I will meet you then, under the mistletoe."

The Very Next Day

The first thing people noticed, on the busy New York street, was the broadsheet newspaper clutched in the small man's hand. That was odd, because his costume would surely have set him apart anywhere outside of Lapland, or wherever winter ruled. It ought to have stood out on a fine day in September like a sore thumb. His coat, which reached over his round belly nearly to his knees, was made of fur, russet red like a deer's hide, and lined with longer white fur. A hood with a long peak lay on his shoulders, revealing wavy white hair worn very long and a shining white moustache and beard that seemed as if they had been growing for centuries, if not decades. His boots of black leather shone like mirrors, as did the silver buckle of his black belt. Normally, they would not expect to see a man dressed as Santa Claus sooner than December, but today everyone in Manhattan felt a bit indulgent and nostalgic.

"Nice outfit," the man in the newspaper kiosk said, glancing up. "Giving the suit an airing today?"

"Why, no," "Santa Claus" said. "This is what I wear all of the time."

The newspaper vendor shrugged. A harmless nut, but he looked like the real thing, and that made him feel good. He pushed the flat wool cap back on his head and scratched his scalp. Like a boy again.

"Just in town for the day?"

Santa slapped his chest with his hand and looked up at the tall buildings—the tallest in the world. He felt a thrill to see them. "Why, yes! It's a fine city. I never do get to see them in daylight. Always by moonlight or starlight." He glanced down at the paper in his hand.

The vendor nodded toward the newspaper. "Nice piece of writin' there, ain't it?"

Santa nodded. "Truly. I would be convinced, if I were a child."

Something in the way the old man said the last word sounded disappointed. The newsman gave him an encouraging grin.

"Everyone was, if you ask me. Wanna copy of today's paper?"

"No, thank you," the old man said. "I haven't done with this one yet." He folded it up and put it in his pocket. Then he eyed the newsman, counted the gaps in his smile. "You should take better care of your teeth, you know."

The newspaper vendor felt his face go red. "Don't you make personal comments to me, geezer!"

"But you promised me," "Santa" said. "In your letter. If I brought you that stuffed leather horse, you'd clean your teeth every day, just as your mother asked you."

The newsman's mouth dropped open. "But that was forty years ago!"

"A promise is a promise."

"Yeah." He ran his tongue over the remaining teeth in his mouth. "I will, Santa. I really will. Thanks. And thanks for the horse. I really loved it. I gave it to my first daughter when she was born."

"You were a good boy, Louis," Santa said, offering his free hand for a shake. Louis clutched the leather glove.

How absolutely marvelous that he knew everything there was about a child just by looking at him, Santa thought as he turned away from the wondering eyes. Then he paused, confused. *How* did *I know all that?*

What was going on inside his head was not nearly so amazing as what was outside it. New York was a place of wonders! Santa gazed around him in wonder, taking it all in. Men and women wore clothing made of the most exquisite fabrics, soft and evenly woven and dyed in colors that had heretofore existed only in rainbows and spring meadows. Gentlemen in brilliant white linen jackets tipped their flat straw hats to ladies whose long, shining hair was piled up in a pumpkin shape on their heads. The streets themselves were surprisingly clean. Men pushing barrels on wheels stopped to sweep and scoop up refuse deposited by horses.

He had expected to be overwhelmed by the odor of sewage and rotten vegetation on top of the smell of coal fires that filled the air. Instead, there was a new scent, a sharp burning scent. Horses drew carriages through the streets as well as on narrow metal rails, but over his head and in the windows of the many, many shops, tiny lights encased in glass shone. They were not candles, they were light bulbs. The smell was that of *electricity*. Such things did not exist in many places yet, that he knew, but this was a city that had to have everything new as soon as possible. He walked between tall, stone buildings with shining bronze doors. Fantastic, swooping designs were pressed into them. Art Nouveau, they called it. Beautiful. New World, new art. New music poured from the doors of clubs.

From a point at the very tip of the island, he saw in the harbor a magnificent statue, a woman facing away from him, with a torch in her hand raised in welcome. He did not have to see her face to know that she was Liberty herself. She had been a gift. Santa had not given her, but he knew when something had been tendered with love or respect. He felt as if *he* had been given a present, to see something that represented such an ideal.

Children who had been looking out into the harbor noticed the small man in their midst. They broke away from their parents and came tearing toward him.

"Santa!" "Santa Claus!" "Sinterklaas!"

They danced around him, laughing, and he shared their delight. Little girls in bows tied on top of their heads, boys in knee pants, urchins without shoes. They hugged him, tugged on his coat, tried to clamber into his arms, though he was scarcely taller than they were. They felt in his pockets and came up with handfuls of hard candies wrapped in bright cellophane. Their eyes were alight with happiness.

"What are you doing here?" one asked.

"Where are your reindeer? Can I say hello to Dancer?"

"Mama said you would bring me a train for Christmas if I am good. Will you?"

"Well, well, well, we will see!" Santa said, chucking a chin here and offering a hug there. "Are you helping your mother with the chores? She needs help now that your new brother has arrived."

"Aw," said Steven, the boy who wanted the train. "I *guess*."

"Good for you! Then you will be on my good list for this Christmas!"

Steven glowed with pride.

With every child's question, Santa felt himself growing stronger and more alive. How marvelous it was to interact with the little ones whom he usually glimpsed asleep in their beds if at all. He knew of the dreams they had and wishes they made. They were a joy awake. He loved to be with them all.

They all knew everything about him, and because they did, he knew everything about them. Glynnis had a lisp that made her friends tease her. Fridur had recently come to the United States with his parents from the Netherlands. They were poor, but making their way. His mother took in washing, and his father worked on the docks. Evelyn was from a wealthy family, but her brother had just died of typhoid. All of them had been good except Mick. He was cruel to animals. Santa regarded him with stern pity. He did not have to say anything. The boy shrank away from his bright gaze. He knew too much about Santa to imagine that his sins were hidden from him.

What did Santa know about himself? More memories came to him as he spoke with the children. He lived far away, where it was cold. They were unclear as to where, as each of them had a different idea. He drove a sleigh with reindeer. He made toys. Not all by himself. Little men helped him. They loaded the sleigh on Christmas Eve, and he drove all over the world. He brought toys for good children, and punished bad ones—no, he brought rocks and coal for bad ones. His assistants did not beat children any more. He was glad of that.

"How do you go all the way around the world in just one night?" a boy with big brown eyes asked. His name was Julian. He was ten, and his grandfather had been a war hero.

"My reindeer are very swift," Santa said. "I have worked out the very best route possible. I am always home by dawn." He knew in his soul that it was absolutely true. The other children nodded eagerly.

"But it's impossible to go to every house with children! There are millions of them!

"It takes magic," Santa explained. "You do believe in magic, don't you?"

Julian crossed his arms. "My daddy said that magic doesn't exist. Just science."

"Isn't there room for both in your heart?"

"But you think with your head, not your heart!"

Santa tapped his own temple. "A smart person knows that he should listen to all the parts of his body."

"Who brings you presents, Santa?"

What a good child, that little girl with long yellow braids tied with blue ribbons. Her name was Caroline. She was just eight.

He stroked her hair, marveling at the silky strands. "Why, you do, children. Every smile, every laugh, every 'thank you' is a gift to me."

"That's funny," she said.

"Why do you believe in me?" he asked. "Is it because of this newspaper article?" He showed them the paper from his pocket. Caroline shook her head.

"Oh, no, I always believed in you. Daddy and Mama and Granddad and Gamma say you are real. But I know I heard you in my parlor last Christmas."

Santa remembered, the memory as vivid in his mind as in hers. "When I left you the doll with golden braids, just like yours."

"Yes!"

"So you was just pretendin' to be asleep!" Mick said.

"No, she was really asleep," Santa explained. "She was dreaming. You can hear me in your dreams. Sometimes you can see me, too." He knew that Mick had. The boy had also dreamt of those helpers that punished bad children. Mick believed, even if he didn't behave.

"Come away, sweetheart," said a slender woman in a white shirtwaist, a tiny blue jacket trimmed with maroon braids and a graceful, long blue skirt that swept the pavement. A tiny hat made of feathers was perched upon her hair. "We must get you to school."

Caroline didn't want to let go of his hand. "But, Mommy, it's Santa Claus!"

Mary, that was her name, detached Caroline's hand. "No, sweetheart, just someone dressed up as him." She looked Santa up and down. Her expression was disapproving. "Good day, sir."

"Good day," Santa said. He watched them go, feeling his heart grow heavy.

Mary thought he wasn't real. Her mind embraced something hard that was pushing her away from the belief that she had had as a child herself. Though she stopped short of telling Caroline Santa Claus wasn't real, she ... doubted. He felt his flesh thinning on his bones. Skepticism ate away at his very body. It hurt. He put a hand to his aching ribs. He had never felt pain before. It was unpleasant.

"Don't worry," Evelyn said, slipping her hand into his. She looked up trustingly into his eyes. "I believe in you."

"Thank you, my dear," Santa said, touched.

So did her father, who tipped his hat as he came to retrieve his daughter. Peter's eyes were filled with wonder.

That abated the ache a bit better, but it didn't rebuild Santa's flesh completely. The children drifted away, some to school, others to hang around the waterfront. They were happy he was there. They felt comfort in his presence. They did him good as well.

He lit his pipe and took a deep breath of the fragrant tobacco smoke. Life felt good. He must see more of the city, and speak to more children.

As he was turning away, an urchin on the docks who had hung back from the group ran up and kicked him in the shin.

"I hate you!" he said, fury in his filthy face. "All I wanted was a pocketknife! You didn' leave me nothin' but a dirty piece of coal. Said I been a bad boy!"

"But you had been bad last year, Donald," Santa said. His leg hurt, but it meant that the boy believed in him. "I was disappointed in you. I hope not to be this year."

Donald was too angry to see the connection. He spat on the ground and ran away, but he glanced back to see if Santa was watching him. The adults went about their business, carrying loads and checking off lists. They were too busy on a work day to pay attention to what children cared about. But, truly, what could be more important?

Children looked at him and knew what they saw. They knew he existed. It was only when they peeked around the newel post and saw their parents placing gifts under the tree that they began to understand that he had not come to their house, that the presents had a much more prosaic origin. But he was here now. They could see him. All the things that they knew about him were true. He had reindeer and a sleigh and a workshop. He would get back to work as soon as he could, if only they didn't stop believing in him.

But a child had doubted his existence, because other children had told her he *wasn't* real. He read the newspaper column again. His heart squeezed with regret.

No! He was real! Life was joy. Life was precious. All those rooftops, his trips around the world every year high in the sky on his reindeer-drawn sleigh never engendered fear in him. He did not fear the tight confines of chimneys, though his handsome fur suit often was the worse for all the soot. But it must be true. He had never existed before. And something was trying to push him out again now that he had been made real. Science. Science denied him.

And it was all around him. Twinkling lights that were not made of fire, encased in light bubbles of glass. Everywhere he walked, he saw fascinating new inventions, wonders in themselves. Human beings defied the darkness, pushed back ignorance, spread knowledge in new ways. They had chained the lightning. Small wonder that they had pushed from them that little comfort of someone giving them simple gifts out of love. Was he no longer relevant?

Santa did not want to go away again. He could not imagine anything more wonderful than being here among people, seeing how they lived, how they felt. Cold fear made a knot in his belly. He did not recall what it was like before he had appeared on that street corner. The thought of not existing again worried him.

It was the nature of life to want to remain alive. What did he have to do to stay that way?

As he walked through the bustling city, he saw no place where he belonged. He touched upon the lives of people only once a year. Here and now he was misplaced in time.

I'm not satisfied to exist only one day, he thought.

Peddlers pulling carts glanced up and saw him. Women doing their day's shopping noticed him. Men in waistcoats, collars and ties peered his way. Most smiled, then looked away hastily. A few stared openly. He greeted them with a cheerful wave. They saw, they hoped to believe, and they doubted.

The next time a man caught his eye and turned away with a sheepish expression, Santa hurried after him. He was panting by the time he caught up with the man at a busy corner. He took his arm. The man, in his late thirties, prosperous, with a lush mustache waxed at the ends to curl upward, clad in a fine wool coat reaching to his knees, a silk waistcoat adorned with a heavy gold chain and a top hat made of silk, shied like a horse at the sight of the little man in fur.

"Do you know who I am?" Santa asked. "You do, I can see it in you."

The words came to Alfred's lips unwillingly. "You are Santa Claus," he said.

"But you only think I look like Santa, don't you. What would it take for you to believe that I *am* Santa Claus?"

Alfred shook his arm loose. "You are nothing but a strange old man in a fur suit. You are mad. You need the new psychoanalysis to help you. Good day!" He rushed off, skirting under the nose of the policeman directing traffic and a goods van loaded with clanking cans of milk.

Santa was, briefly, all of those things that the man said, but the rest of the millions of children who did believe in him dispelled the bad and left the good. Alfred did not totally disbelieve, that Santa could see in his heart, but he doubted so much that he had to deny belief completely. How very sad. Santa's pain returned, eating the muscles in his legs. His cheeks began to feel sunken. He felt himself slipping away. He looked around for help. Few people would meet his eyes.

Doubt was his enemy. He must banish doubt, and continue to live.

One didn't have to prove an article of faith to children; one only had to let them believe. Adults need proof. No, adults needed to believe the child within, who still knows there is a Santa Claus.

The only proof, if proof it was, that he was worthwhile lay in the palm of his hand. He read the words again, and they filled his heart with joy and hope. That reply to a simple child's query was a complex construction. It had brought him into existence for the first time.

But who had written it? His greatest ally and savior in this city of modern wonders was the man who had penned these moving words.

He returned to the kiosk on 34th Street and held out the sheet of newsprint. "Louis, how do I find the man who wrote this?"

"At the *New York Sun*," Louis said. He pointed up the long street that intersected with 34th. "That's Broadway. Take it to Chambers and look for the clock."

"Thank you, my friend."

Louis grinned. His teeth looked cleaner already. "My pleasure, Santa. He's gonna be really surprised to see you."

O O O

"I would like to meet the man who wrote this," Santa told the stout uniformed porter at the bronze and glass door of the newspaper office.

The big man sneered down at him from his great height. "I bet you do. A lot of crazies came out of the woodwork after yesterday's editorial." He eyed Santa skeptically. "Your outfit's a lot better than most of 'em. You can go ahead, if you want. It'll give everyone a good laugh."

He passed Santa along to a copyboy, who brought him to the city desk editor, who laughed hard enough to attract everyone within a three-desk radius. They all chuckled at Santa, but they agreed with the door porter, that it would be great fun to send him in to Mr. Church.

The doubters in the *Sun* office greatly outnumbered the believers. Santa could hardly push his way through the agony that ate away at him. It was only the uniformed black porter who took his arm who made it possible for him to get up the stairs to the third floor. His strength was in rags by the time he reached the female receptionist at the desk outside the editor's office in the busy newsroom. She regarded him with sympathy but no understanding. Margaret had always been that way, Santa knew. It would do him no good to tell her so.

"Mr. Church is in a meeting. You may wait." She gestured to a hard-backed chair against the wall.

If he had thought the streets of New York were noisy, they were silent as a winter's night compared with the newsroom. Typewriters clattered under the fingers of men and women alike. Copyboys, many no older than ten, ran up and back with their arms laden with sheets of paper. Men shouted over the din at one another. Under his feet Santa felt the thrum of the presses, the heartbeat of the *Sun*.

At last, the door swung open. Two men in short plaid jackets emerged, shoving notebooks into their pockets. They eyed Santa speculatively as they went by. Matthew felt a wave of nostalgia, but Henry saw only an old man in a red fur coat. Santa understood. Henry covered the new scientific advances. He was on his way to meet Mr. Westinghouse. Matthew wrote about baseball, so he maintained faith and hope in a way that was almost childlike. Though he would have died on the rack before he would have admitted it to a living soul. He was off to see a Giants game that day at the Polo Grounds.

"Go in," Margaret told Santa.

"Well, Mr. *Claus*," Frank Church said, putting out a hand to Santa. He was a tall, spare man with bushy eyebrows. "My colleagues told me you were here." He smiled, lifting the corners of his luxurious mustache a trifle. "Please, have a seat. I can give you a few moments. What may I do for you?"

"It is about your editorial," Santa said, producing the newspaper.

Mr. Church looked amused. "Yes, I assumed that was so. What about it?"

"Well, to be straightforward, it seems to have brought me into existence. Your words moved me deeply. I assume that they moved thousands of your fellow New Yorkers to belief, and for that I thank you. So many people feeling the truth of your eloquent plea has caused me to appear in their midst. I rather like it, and want to continue to *be*. I have come to ask for your help."

Frank nodded. "So you want me to believe that you are the true Santa Claus. Who sent you? Haley at the *Times*? It'd be just like him."

Santa found Church's skepticism to be perfectly natural. He was a grown man who had seen tragedy and horror in his life, yet he felt Frank's desperate hope to believe in the fairy tale that he had written about just the other day. He had grown to be an adult, yet a spark of faith and wonder remained.

"Mr. Haley did not send me. I am Santa Claus," Santa said, reassuringly. "You should know what to look for. You expressed it most beautifully in your column."

"I . . ." Frank did not know what to say. "It was for the sake of that child, you know. She ought to be allowed to remain a child as long as possible."

"I do understand that," Santa said. "But I should not have to explain to you how important it is for science and simplicity to coexist. One must not fear to be a little child again, when times of wonder are at hand."

"You are not a simple thing, Mr. Claus," Frank said. "You seem to be well-educated and a philosopher to boot, but I think I have to decline. I'm not equal to the task." Frank's defenses were growing. Santa felt Logic and Science teaming up to push him out of the world.

"I can prove my reality to you, but that would defeat the purpose, would it not?" Santa searched Frank's face. "I think that I have my answer."

The pains spread across his whole body now. His back and sides ached. His nerves were exposed, and his soul was starting to spread out again across the universe. How sad that he should not be able to enjoy this world a little longer. He fetched a breath, but it caught on the pain.

"Shall I call for the nurse?" Frank asked. He was not a heartless man, merely mortal and conflicted, as any human being was.

"No, it will pass, as I will. I thought you could help me to live longer." Santa smiled. "I should be grateful for the day—and I am. It's a gift I never knew. When one is an ideal, one's feet never really touch the pavement, you see. I have seen electric lights, and liberty, and the joy in little children's faces. It is enough."

"There isn't a touch of irony in you, is there?" Frank said, his brow drawn into a furrow. "How I wish I could be that way."

"You have been, at times. As you were when you wrote that lovely piece. It is oblique suggestion, not proof, but I could sense your whole heart in it. You have always been that idealist. I admire that in you. That is why you chose journalism as your career. You believe in truth. You'd rather be honest than liked."

"You were briefed very thoroughly about me," Frank said, doubtful once more. "Was it my wife told you my story? My brother?"

Santa smiled. "One of the things that I discovered today that people know about me is that I can see into their hearts. It is true. I … I was not going to do this, because it will spoil your natural faith, but it will quell your skepticism." He reached into his pocket and took from it a carved wooden lamb. He set it on Frank Church's desk. It was painted white and had a blue ribbon around its neck.

"You wanted this when you were very small, when you saw it in the Christ Child's crèche. Your mother told you that it was not right for you to take it. I couldn't give it to you then, but you shall have it now."

Frank's face went through a rainbow's worth of expressions, from outrage to astonishment to grief to outright wonder. He took the lamb and ran a finger on its knobbly head. "No one knew that. No one could have remembered that." He stood up. "I shall do whatever you wish, Santa. But come with me now! I shall take you to visit little Virginia. She's the one who precipitated me into writing my piece. She will be delighted beyond reason to see that she was not wrong to believe."

Santa held up a hand. "Oh, no, Frank. She's the one person that does not need to meet me. You convinced her very thoroughly indeed with your poetry. Her friends are a trifle embarrassed that they doubted, as are their parents. It's you who needed to be reassured. And me."

Church's eyes widened. "Why you? You are Santa Claus."

"I am what all of you have made me. If you cease to believe, and you just proved how easy a thing that is to do, then I do not exist. I celebrate the birth of the Christ Child. How I do that and what people expect of me differs from person to person. Some resent me. Some hate me. What you wrote will help me be in this world for a little longer. I want to exist."

"You shall," Church said, his thin face passionate. "You live forever."

"So you said in your lovely letter, sir. But these are New Yorkers. I feel as if I am fading already. No matter what we do here today, I cannot last. The shared belief that you caused is passing away. By tomorrow, I shall be a memory again, though a cherished one, I hope."

Frank looked aghast. "No! I believe in you."

Santa shook his head. It hurt a little to move. "But you doubt what you see. You cannot help it. It's a natural thing. We cast aside that which does not allow us to walk freely, to explore, to make our own decisions, right or wrong. It is … human. They have to be free to say there is no Santa Claus. But wonder, magic, and love must always be allowed in children's lives. If you help to give them that, and you have, I will always live a little. That will satisfy me. I did not think it would, but it does, because it is what children need. It is better for me to be a dream, to live in that unseen world you spoke of."

"I will always assert the truth of your existence," Frank Church assured him. "The veil to the unseen world is torn asunder, and I see the glory I wished was there."

Santa felt the twinge of doubt that lessened the force of the statement. "Ah, no. You are already wondering if I am making a fool of you. You know the Santa you believed in would not do so. Your Santa keeps your letters, dreams, and wishes to himself. But you needn't believe me completely. Keep being a cynic, so you can prevent others being fooled. The moment you don't doubt, then you stop being of use as a newsman, and I would not ruin a distinguished career such as the one you have built for yourself."

Church laughed. "I feel sad, you know. You have given me the best Christmas gift of my life, and I do not mean the lamb. I wish I could give you what you want."

Santa laid his finger beside his round little nose. "Ah, but you have. You gave me this day. To be manifested and see what I mean to people makes me wiser than I was. But let us smoke a pipe together and talk. Tell me about this wonderful city. Then, when the time is right, I shall depart, without regrets."

Frank Church smiled. "Up the chimney?" he asked, with a nod toward the fireplace in the corner.

Santa laughed, his belly jiggling up and down with merriment. "Since that is what you truly wish as your gift, it would be my pleasure."

About the Author

Jody Lynn Nye writes fantasy and science fiction books and short stories. Since 1987 she has published over 45 books and more than 120 short stories, including epic fantasies, contemporary humorous fantasy, humorous military science fiction, and edited three anthologies. She collaborated with Anne McCaffrey on a number of books, including the New York Times bestseller, *Crisis on Doona.* She also wrote eight books with Robert Asprin, and continues both Asprin's Myth-Adventures series and Dragons series. Her newest humorous military SF series is the Lord Thomas Kinago Adventures, the most recent of which is *Fortunes of the Imperium* (Baen Books). *The Magic Touch* is a part of the same world of Jody's other well-known contemporary humorous fantasy series, Mythology, recently republished by WorldFire Press. A new novel about the Fairy Godmothers' Union will shortly be published in *Wishing On a Star* (Arc Manor Press), as part of the Stellar Guild series, accompanied by a novella by newcomer Angelina Adams.

Jody's other recent books are *Myth-Quoted* (Ace Books); an e-collection of cat stories, *Cats Triumphant!* (Event Horizon); *Dragons Run* (fourth in the Dragons series) and *Launch Pad*, an anthology of science fiction stories co-edited with Mike Brotherton (WordFire). Jody runs the two-day intensive writers' workshop at DragonCon, and she and her husband, Bill Fawcett are the book reviewers for *Galaxy's Edge Magazine.*

IF YOU LIKED …

If you liked *Circle of Celebrations,* you might also enjoy:

A Fantastic Holiday Season

A Fantastic Holiday Season 2: The Gift of Stories

Other WordFire Press Titles by Jody Lynn Nye

The Magic Touch

Strong Arm Tactics

Mythology 101

Mythology Abroad

Higher Mythology

Advanced Mythology

www.ingramcontent.com/pod-product-compliance
Lightning Source LLC
Chambersburg PA
CBHW030337310726
48979CB00001B/77

9781680575774